"Our Marriage Will Be Companionable With A Progression Toward Intimacy When It Seems Appropriate."

Daniella's tone wavered, just a touch, and was coupled with a glint in her eyes he couldn't interpret. "Like we discussed."

His exact words. And suddenly Leo wished he could take it all back.

"We'll have separate bedrooms for now. Take things slowly," he said.

That had been his intent from the beginning and seemed even more necessary given the unexpected chemistry between them. It should solve everything.

So why did the back of his throat burn with inexplicable disappointment?

* * *

Matched to a Billionaire is part of the Happily Ever After, Inc. trilogy: Their business is makeovers and matchmaking, but love doesn't always go according to plan!

* * *

If you're on Twitter,
tell us what you think of Harlequin Desire!
#harlequindesire

Dear Reader,

I love to dress up! I especially can't resist beautiful shoes—there's a certain kind of magic in the right pair. I also firmly believe in the magic of true love, and that's why I continually retell the Cinderella story in my books.

In this version, the heroine, Daniella, just wants to take care of her sick mother. She signs on with a unique matchmaking agency that performs Cinderella-style makeovers, turning her into the society wife our billionaire, Leo, requested. It was supposed to be a marriage of convenience, but Daniella's fairy godmother has different plans for this perfectly matched couple. This is a modern-day fairy tale absent a ball and a pumpkin, but I wouldn't dare leave out the midnight transformation.

I've always wanted to write a series of connected stories, because as a reader, I love revisiting beloved characters and anticipating the stories to come of other characters. So I'm thrilled to bring you the first story in the Happily Ever After, Inc. trilogy in which three couples find love where they least expect it.

If you enjoy this book starring Daniella and Leo, I hope you'll pick up the next two! I would love to hear from you. Drop me a note at www.katcantrell.com.

Thanks for reading!

Kat Cantrell

MATCHED TO A BILLIONAIRE

KAT CANTRELL

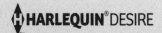

Recycling programs
for this product may
not exist in your area.

ISBN-13: 978-0-373-73328-6

MATCHED TO A BILLIONAIRE

This edition published by arrangement with Harlequin Books S.A.

For questions and comments about the quality of this book, please contact us
at CustomerService@Harlequin.com.

® and TM are trademarks of Harlequin Enterprises Limited or its corporate
affiliates. Trademarks indicated with ® are registered in the United States Patent and
Trademark Office, the Canadian Intellectual Property Office and in other countries.

Printed in U.S.A.

KAT CANTRELL

read her first Harlequin novel in third grade and has
been scribbling in notebooks since she learned to spell.
What else would she write but romance? She majored in
literature, officially with the intent to teach, but somehow
ended up buried in middle management in corporate
America, until she became a stay-at-home mom and full-
time writer.

Kat, her husband and their two boys live in north Texas.
When she's not writing about characters on the journey
to happily-ever-after, she can be found at a soccer game,
watching the TV show *Friends* or listening to '80s music.

Kat was the 2011 Harlequin So You Think You Can Write
winner and a 2012 RWA Golden Heart finalist for best
unpublished series contemporary manuscript.

To Jennifer Hayward, because you're always there for me. And because you liked Leo from the beginning.

One

Leo Reynolds wished he could marry his admin. It would make life so much simpler.

Unfortunately, she was already married and nearly twice his age. Plus, women didn't stick around once they figured out he worked a hundred hours a week on a consistent basis. Loneliness was the price of catapulting Reynolds Capital Management into the big leagues of the venture capital game.

"You're a life saver, Mrs. Gordon." Leo shot her a grateful smile and leaned back in his chair.

His laptop was refusing to speak to the printer and a critical document had gotten caught in the middle of the dispute. The signed hard copy now in his hand was due to Garrett Engineering on the other side of Dallas in less than an hour.

"I'd hardly call printing a proposal saving your life." Mrs. Gordon glanced at her watch in a deliberate gesture designed to point out the time. "It's late and it's Friday. Take Jenna to that new restaurant in Victory Park and let me handle the proposal. Relax for once. It'll be good for you."

Leo grimaced as a ping of remorse bloomed and faded. "Jenna and I split up. She's already seeing someone else."

Hopefully, the new relationship would make her happy. She deserved a man who could shower her with attention and affection. He regretted not being able to give her what she wanted, but it would be patently unfair to let Jenna keep hoping he'd ever become a man capable of focusing on a relationship. As a result, he'd lost a comfortable companion.

"Of course she is. It's not like she ever saw *you*." Mrs. Gordon crossed her arms and looked down her nose at Leo with a tsk. "Now who are you going to take to the museum dedication?"

Leo groaned. He'd conveniently forgotten about that, but it wasn't as if he could skip the dedication. The new children's museum in the Dallas Arts District bore his name, after all, since he'd donated the money to build it. "You're free next Saturday, aren't you?"

Mrs. Gordon cackled as though Leo had been joking. "One of these days, I'm going to say yes when you ask me out and really mess with you. If Jenna's not in the picture, find another woman. They seem to be pretty thick on the ground."

Yeah, he tripped over women on a regular basis who would like to go out with him. Or at least they thought they did, right up until they realized they wouldn't be satisfied with what little time and attention he could give. It never took very long to reach that point.

A vague hollow feeling invaded his gut, one he'd experienced more and more lately. He'd written it off as an increased urgency to hit that elusive, unachieved mark of success. But now that it had happened during a discussion about his personal life, he wasn't so convinced.

"I hate dating." *And small talk.* That getting-to-know-you period took time and energy he didn't care to expend. Reynolds Capital Management came first. Always.

"That's because you don't do it often enough."

Here they went, off on her favorite subject. She never got tired of scolding him about the lack of a permanent female in his life.

"Have you been talking to my mother again?"

"We went to lunch Tuesday, as a matter of fact. She says hi." Mrs. Gordon raised her eyebrows and planted guilt simultaneously, as Leo was sure she intended. He got it. He should call his mother. And date eligible women.

Problem was, he not only hated dating, he also hated constantly standing up dates and disappointing women who deserved better. But he liked companionship and, well, he *was* a guy—sex was nice, too. Why couldn't the perfect woman fall in his lap so he could focus on work?

"It is late," Leo said in what was no doubt a transparent attempt to change the subject. "Why don't *you* go home and I'll take the proposal to Garrett?"

He had until five o'clock to get it to Garrett Engineering, formally expressing his interest in doing business with them.

What Steve Jobs was to cell phones, Tommy Garrett was to internal combustion engines. Or would be, as soon as funding was in place. Garrett had invented a revolutionary modification to increase the gas mileage of a standard car engine and Leo intended to be Garrett's venture capital firm of choice. The partnership would net a sizable, long-term profit for both men, and Leo could do what he did best— pull strings behind the scenes.

If Leo won the deal.

No, not *if. When.*

Leo would never rest until his company hit that sweet spot of security, where longevity was a given, not a question mark. His first million hadn't done it. Neither had the first eight figures, because his profits went straight back into leveraged investments that wouldn't pay off until some point in the future. So he didn't rest.

"Since you've scared off yet another female with your dogged determination to work yourself into an early grave, be my guest." Mrs. Gordon waved her approval for Leo to deliver the proposal. "I filled up your car with gas this morning. It wouldn't kill you to glance at the gauge once in a while."

"Thanks. You're too good to me. By the way," Leo threw in as Mrs. Gordon pulled her handbag from a desk drawer,

"I was thinking of having a gathering at my house to wine and dine Tommy Garrett. If I ask very nicely, would you plan it?"

"It's not my job to be your stand-in wife." Mrs. Gordon firmed her mouth, which meant she had a lot more to say but didn't know how to do so tactfully. In the eight years she'd been keeping him sane, he'd seen that look a lot.

With a half laugh, Leo said, "Of course not. That's not part of your job description."

Except it had the ring of uncomfortable truth. When his hair grew too long, Mrs. Gordon scheduled a haircut. His mother's birthday—Mrs. Gordon picked out the gift. The wine-and-dine request had been a bit of a blurred line, but based on the set of Mrs. Gordon's mouth, he'd pretty well turned the line into a trapezoid.

Mrs. Gordon shut down her computer for the night. "Well, it should be part of someone's job description."

"What, like a party planner?" Maybe he should hire a professional in some capacity, which wouldn't cover all his social obligations. But it was better than nothing.

"Like a girlfriend. Or someone who might actually still be around in six weeks. Hire a wife," she said with a nod. "You need a good woman to take care of you outside of the office. Ask *her* to glance at your gas gauge. She can schmooze Garrett and make sure your life is running smoothly. Keep you warm at night."

Her eyebrows waggled but Leo barely noticed.

Hire a wife.

Could you even do such a thing? It seemed too perfect a solution.

He had no time—or the desire—to sift through women until he found one he liked but who also wouldn't expect him to be available. Reynolds Capital Management did not manage itself. His employees and partners depended on him.

A wife couldn't leave him with no notice. It was the ultimate security.

Leo would have a permanent companion to help fill that occasional hollow feeling, one with no hidden agenda involving his assets and connections. They'd both know from the get-go what to expect—stability. There'd be no hard feelings when she realized he hadn't been kidding about giving 100 percent to his company, leaving nothing left over for her.

All or nothing. Commitment was Leo's kryptonite. Once he latched on to something, he gave it everything and then some. Early on, he'd realized that trait was inherited and tried not to make the same mistakes as his father.

Then he'd met Carmen, who taught him the true depths of his weaknesses, and how easily one obsession could become the center of his existence. He practiced putting everything but the goal aside until it was second nature.

Love or success. His personality didn't allow for both and after clawing his way out of the ghetto, he refused to gamble his future.

If he had an understanding wife, work and his personal life would remain completely separate. And best of all, Leo would never have to engage in small talk with a new woman or experience that sharp pang of guilt over canceling on one ever again.

Leo tugged on his suit jacket and hand delivered the proposal to Garrett's people in their tiny downtown office. It wouldn't be tiny for long. Investors far and wide were clamoring to get in on the ground floor with Garrett's technology. Once the company went public, its worth would shoot to legendary status.

Leo had to land the deal with Tommy Garrett, and the wine-and-dine thing would be a fantastic opportunity to solidify his chances. A wife could handle the logistics, leaving Leo to engage in uninterrupted dialogue with Garrett about what Reynolds Capital could do for him that no one else could. His offer to Garrett didn't expire for several weeks. He had plenty of time to get a wife in place.

When Leo returned to his darkened office, he sat at his

laptop. Within fifteen minutes, Google provided a potential answer to the question of how to hire a wife. He'd had to wade through all the cleaning services and concierge services, then a few distasteful escort services, to find the definitive solution.

A matchmaking service.

Yes. Of course. It was not what he'd had in mind when he started the quest. Actually, he hadn't been sure *what* he'd intended to find. But this was an intriguing answer. Leo had always thought he'd get married one day, when he could afford to transfer his energy to a relationship. Yet here he was on the downside of thirty-five and Reynolds Capital Management still took all of his focus. All of his time.

He stared at the logo for EA International. The website was professional and tasteful, with earth tones and a classic font. Most importantly, this particular matchmaker catered to exclusive clients, promising discretion and a money-back guarantee. Guarantees warmed Leo's heart.

The tagline said it all—*Let us help you find "the one."*

Presumably, "the one" for Leo would fit all his qualifications. EA International would do the screening, the interviewing, the background checks, and ultimately filter out candidates who were looking for some mystical connection. Love didn't pay the bills, and Leo would never allow the power to be turned off on his family, the way his own father had.

It was brilliant. The matchmaker would do everything required to find Leo a wife. One he could never disappoint. All he had to do was make a phone call.

Then, with that settled, he could get back to work.

Daniella White had dreamed of her wedding since the first time she'd created crayon invitations to a ceremony starring Mr. Fourpaws as the tattered velveteen groom and herself as the fairy-tale bride wrapped in dingy sheets. Someday she'd wear a beautiful dress of delicate lace and silver heels. The guests would receive heavy card-stock invitations with a vellum overlay and eat a three-tiered French vanilla cake with fondant flowers.

Best of all, a handsome husband-to-be would wait for her at the end of a church aisle, wearing a tender smile. Later that night, the love of her life would sweep her away to a romantic honeymoon somewhere exotic and breathtaking. Theirs would be a marriage of grand passion and enduring love.

When her real wedding day finally arrived, Dannie could never have envisioned it would involve a groom she'd never met in person. Or that in a few minutes, she'd be marrying Leo Reynolds in the living room of a matchmaker's house in North Dallas, with only a handful of guests in attendance.

"What do you think, Mom?" Dannie beamed at her mother in the cheval mirror and straightened a three-quarter-length sleeve. A dress of any sort usually appealed to Dannie, but this unadorned ecru one would be her wedding dress and she wanted to love it. She didn't. But she'd make the best of it, like always.

EA International's sophisticated computer program had matched her with businessman Leo Reynolds and he expected a wife with a certain refinement—one who dressed the part, acted the part, lived the part. Dannie had spent the past month under the matchmaker's intensive tutelage to become exactly right for that part.

Dannie's mother coughed profusely, hand to her chest as if she'd clear the scar tissue from her lungs through sheer will alone. "You're beautiful, baby," she said when she'd recovered. "Every bit a proper wife. I'm so proud of what you've accomplished."

Yeah, it was really hard to put my name in a database. Dannie bit back the comment. She wasn't a smart aleck anymore. No one ever got her jokes anyway.

Two sharp raps at the door shoved Dannie's heart into her throat. Elise Arundel, Dannie's fairy godmother–slash–

matchmaker, popped into the room, her sleek, dark pageboy swinging. "Oh, Dannie. You look lovely."

Dannie smiled demurely. She needed a lot of practice at being demure.

"Thanks to you."

"I didn't pick out that dress." Elise nodded once. "You did. It's perfect for your willowy frame. I've never had anyone who glommed on to cut and style with such natural talent."

"I made up for it by being hopeless with cosmetics." Dannie frowned. Did that seem too outspoken? Ungrateful? That was the problem with changing your personality to become a society wife—nothing came naturally.

Elise's critical eye swept over Dannie's face and she dismissed the comment with a flick of her manicured hand. "You're flawless. Leo's socks will be knocked off."

And there went her pulse again.

The figure in the mirror stared back at her, almost a stranger, but with her dark brown hair and almond-colored eyes. Would Leo be happy with her sophisticated chignon? The erect posture? The scared-to-death woman in the ecru dress? What if he didn't like brunettes?

She was being silly. He'd seen her picture, of course, as she'd seen his. They'd spoken on the phone twice. Their conversations had been pleasant and they'd worked through several important marital issues: they'd allow the intimate side of their relationship to evolve over time, a clarification that had clinched it since he didn't believe he was buying an "exchange of services," and he was open to eventually having children.

Neither of them had any illusions about the purpose of this marriage—a permanent means to an end.

Why was she so nervous about what was essentially an arranged marriage?

Her mother smoothed a hand over Dannie's hair. "Soon you'll be Mrs. Leo Reynolds and all your dreams will come true. For the rest of your life, you'll have the security and companionship I never had." Racking coughs punctuated the sentiment and the ticking clock in Dannie's mind sped up. Pulmonary fibrosis was killing her mother.

Dannie was marrying Leo to save her.

And she'd never forget what she owed him. What she owed Elise.

Her mom was right. Dannie had always dreamed of being a wife and mother and now she was getting that chance. Marriage based on compatibility would provide security for her and her mom. She had no business being sad that security couldn't be based on love.

Maybe love could grow over time, along with intimacy. She'd hang on to that hope.

With a misty smile, Elise opened the door wider. "Leo's waiting for you in front of the fireplace. Here's your bouquet. Simple and tasteful, with orchids and roses, like you requested."

The clutch of flowers nearly wrenched the tears loose from Dannie's eyes. "It's beautiful. Everything is beautiful. I can't thank you enough."

She still couldn't believe Elise had selected *her* for the EA International matchmaking program. When she'd applied, it had all seemed like such a long shot, but what choice did she have? Her mother needed expensive long-term care, which neither of them could afford, so Dannie gladly did whatever her mother needed—doctor's appointments, cooking, cleaning. Her father had left before she'd been born, so it had been the two of them against the world since the beginning.

Unfortunately, employers rarely forgave the amount of time off Dannie required. After being fired from the third job in a row, her situation felt pretty dire. She'd searched in vain for a work-from-home job or one with a flexible schedule. After hours at the library's computer, she'd been about to give up when the ad for EA International caught her eye.

Have you ever dreamed of a different sort of career? Coupled with a picture of a bride, how could she not click on it?

EA International invited women with superior administrative skills, a desire to better themselves and the drive to become "the woman behind the man" to apply for a bold, innovative training program.

Who had better admin skills than someone managing the care of a perpetually ill mother? Without much to lose, Dannie sent her information into the ether and shock of all shocks, got the call.

It was fate that EA International was based in Dallas, where Dannie lived.

Elise polished Dannie until she shone and then matched her with a man who needed an elegant society wife. In exchange for organizing Leo's household and hosting parties, Dannie could take care of her mother without any more financial worries.

A marriage that was little more than a contract seemed a small price to pay.

"You're one of my most successful graduates." Elise handed Dannie the bouquet and shifted a couple of flowers to face the outside. "I predict you'll be one of my most successful matches, as well. You and Leo couldn't be better suited."

Dannie's stomach lurched. She wanted to like him. To enjoy being married. Would she be attracted to him? What if she wasn't? Would the intimate side of their marriage never happen? Maybe she should have insisted they meet first in spite of their mutual agreement not to.

It hardly mattered. Attraction wasn't a factor here, but surely they'd eventually hold a great deal of affection for each other, regardless of what he looked like.

Nose to the bouquet, Dannie inhaled the sweet scent of her wedding flowers. "We have similar goals and both recognize the practicality of this union. I expect we'll be very happy together."

Leo had gobs of money. She'd have been happy with half a gob. That level of wealth intimidated her, but Elise insisted she could handle it. After all, Dannie would have a valued place in his life and she might eventually be the mother of his children. Her training had made it very clear the woman behind the man worked as hard as women in other careers.

"Happy is exactly what you'll be." Elise pinched the clasp of Dannie's necklace, dragging it to the nape of her neck. The open-heart lavaliere hanging from the chain had been a gift from the matchmaker when Dannie agreed to marry Leo. "My computer program is never wrong."

Dannie's mother chimed in. "This is the best kind of match, one that will last forever, because it's based on compatibility, not feelings. It's everything Dannie wants in a marriage."

Dannie forced a nod, though she wished she could disagree, and spared only a passing thought to Rob. She'd been so gaga over him.

Look where that had gotten her—brokenhearted and determined to make over her temperament so no man could call her opinionated and blunt again. She'd screwed up that relationship but good.

She wasn't going to screw up this one. Her mother couldn't afford it.

"Yes," she agreed. "Security and companionship. What else could I possibly ask for?"

Fairy tales were stories about magical solutions to problems and full of people who fell in love, but whose relationships couldn't possibly stand the test of time. In real life, women had to make sacrifices and Dannie was making hers.

Without any further melancholy and ridiculousness, she marched out the door of the room she'd stayed in during her transformation and went to meet her fate on a prayer that she and Leo would at least grow to care for each other. If there was more, great. She'd consider it a bonus.

Her mother and Elise followed. Dannie paused at the top of the sweeping staircase and took in the scene below.

With cheerful optimism, Elise had placed flower arrangements on the mantel and on each side of the fireplace. Dannie's heart fluttered at the thoughtfulness of the woman who had become her friend. A photographer stood at the back of the room, poised to snap memories at a moment's notice, and the gray-haired minister Elise had recommended waited in front of the fireplace.

To his right was Leo Reynolds. Her husband-to-be.

He looked up and met her gaze.

A shock of…something zapped across her shoulders. He looked exactly like his picture, but in person—*hello*. Dark, straight hair brushed his collar and an expensive, well-designed suit encased a masculine body Leo clearly kept in great shape. Classic, smooth features formed a face handsome enough to sell out an entire print run of *GQ* magazine. More Ashley than Rhett, which was appropriate since she'd banished her inner Scarlett O'Hara to a place where the sun didn't shine.

Leo also looked kind, as though he wouldn't hesitate to carry an elderly lady's groceries to the car. Dannie almost snorted. If Leo Reynolds had ever seen the inside of a grocery store, she'd eat her bouquet. He was a busy man and it was a good thing for her that he was, or he wouldn't need a wife.

Not for the first time, she wondered why he'd resorted to a matchmaker. He was good-looking, rich and well-spoken. By all rights, the eligible-woman line should be wrapped around the block.

Eyes on Leo, she descended the stairs with practiced ease—she'd done it in four-inch heels dozens of times and didn't falter today despite the severity of the occasion. In far too few steps, she reached Leo. In her bone-colored pumps, she and Leo were nearly the same height.

She searched his expression as he did the same to her. What did you say to a man you were about to marry but whom you were seeing for the first time in the flesh? *Hey, fancy meeting you here.*

A hysterical giggle nearly slipped out. Not an auspicious start.

"Hello." Well, that should be reasonably safe.

"Hello," Leo returned and smiled, setting off a nice, warm flutter in her chest.

Up close, he was solid and powerful, capable of carrying a baby in one arm and taking out a carjacker with the other. The flutter that thought set off was a little warmer and little more south than the first one. In theory, she'd known Leo equated to safety. But reality was far more... real. And affecting.

They faced front. Nerves locked Dannie's knees and she tried to loosen them without drawing attention. If she pitched over in the middle of her wedding ceremony, Elise would never forgive her.

"Let's begin." The minister raised a Bible in his wrinkled hands and began reciting the vows Leo had insisted Dannie select.

The words flowed from the minister's mouth, sounding completely different aloud than she would have imagined. For better or worse, richer or poorer. None of that really applied, not in the way it did for most couples. Those vows were a call to remember the reasons you fell in love in the first place when marriage got tough.

From her peripheral vision, she tried to catch a glimpse of Leo to see how all this was registering. Suddenly she wished they'd had a few more conversations so she'd know better what he might be thinking.

It had just seemed so unnecessary. Elise wouldn't have allowed her to marry someone awful. Her screening process was diligent and faultless, matching her with Leo on all forty-seven points of the personality profile. So long as he wasn't a criminal or a wife beater, what did it matter if he had a good sense of humor or liked sweeping historical dramas?

"Do you take Leo as your lawfully wedded husband?" the minister intoned.

Dannie cleared her throat. "I do."

With a trembling hand, she slipped a plain platinum band on Leo's finger. Or tried to. She couldn't get it over the knuckle and when he covered her hand with his to assist, she glanced up to meet his blue eyes.

That same odd shock she'd experienced on the stairs rocked her shoulders. It wasn't awareness, but deeper, as if she'd just seen someone she knew but couldn't place.

She shook it off. Nerves. That's all.

Leo repeated, "I do," his voice even and strong. Because he wasn't nervous. Why would he be, with all that masculine confidence?

The platinum band he slid on her finger matched his and winked in the living room's overhead lighting. She stared at it, transfixed by the sheer weight such a simple band added to her hand.

Divorce wasn't an option.

Both she and Leo had indicated a strong belief in honoring commitments in their profiles and it had been the first thing addressed in their phone conversation. Leo had been far too generous in the original prenuptial agreement and she'd refused to marry him without serious alterations, namely that any future children would be provided for but she'd get nothing. In her mind, that was the best way to demonstrate the seriousness of her word.

Leo represented security, not free money. And in exchange for that security, she'd be the wife he needed.

This marriage was a permanent solution to their problems, not a love match. Which was fine by her. Leo would never leave her the way her father had and she'd never have to worry about whether he'd stop loving her if she screwed up.

The minister signaled the end of the short ceremony with the traditional, "You may kiss the bride."

Oh, why had she asked for that part? It was going to be so weird. But it was her *wedding*. Shouldn't she get a kiss from her husband? A kiss to seal their bargain.

Leo turned to her, his expression unreadable. As his lips descended, she closed her eyes. Their mouths touched.

And held for a shimmering moment, launching a typhoon of flutters in her abdomen. Maybe the possibility of having a whole lot more than just affection between them wasn't as remote as she'd thought.

Then he recoiled as if he'd licked a lemon wedge and stepped away.

Their first kiss. How…disappointingly brief, with a hint of possible sparks she'd had no time to enjoy. Hadn't he felt it? Obviously not.

Her mother and Elise clapped, gathering around her and Leo to gush with congratulations.

Dannie swallowed. What had she expected—Leo would magically transform from a venture capitalist into Prince Charming? Elise's computer program had matched her with the perfect husband, one who would take care of her and her mother and treat Dannie well. She should be happy they'd have a fulfilling partnership.

She should *not* be thinking about how Leo might kiss her if they'd met under different circumstances. If they were getting married because they'd fallen in love, and during the ceremony he'd slid her a sizzling glance that said he couldn't wait for the honeymoon.

She shouldn't be dwelling on it, but the thought wouldn't fade—what would his calm blue eyes look like when they were hot with passion?

Two

Daniella stood by the door with her hands clasped and chin down. Leo's new wife was refined and unassuming, exactly as he had specified. What he had not expected was to find her picture had lied. And it was a monstrous lie of epic proportions.

She wasn't girl-next-door attractive, as he'd believed. This woman he'd married radiated sensuous energy, as if her spirit was leashed behind a barrier of skin that could barely contain it. If that leash ever broke—look out.

She wasn't merely gorgeous; in person, Daniella defied description.

The stuff of poetry and Michael Bublé songs. If one was inclined toward that sort of thing.

Even her name was exotic and unusual. He couldn't stop looking at her. He couldn't stop thinking about the way-too-short kiss he'd broken off because it felt like the beginning of something that would take a very long time to finish. His entire body buzzed in response to that concentrated energy it badly wanted to explore.

What was he going to do with a woman like *that?*

"I'm ready to leave whenever you are, Leo." Her voice, soft but self-assured, carried across the foyer of Ms. Arundel's house.

He was going to take her home. Regardless of having *distraction* written all over her, they were married.

His recon skills clearly needed help. Why hadn't he met

her first? Because he'd dotted as many *i*'s and crossed as many *t*'s as possible before fully committing to this idea. Or so he'd thought. Leo had spoken with other satisfied clients of EA International and then personally met with Elise Arundel several times. He had confidence in her ability to find the right match, and the thorough background check Ms. Arundel had supplied confirmed her choice.

Daniella White was the perfect woman to be his wife.

Their phone calls had sealed the deal. He'd recognized her suitability immediately and everything fell into place. Why wait to marry when they were like-minded and neither cared if there was any attraction between them? It was better to get on with it.

If he had it to do over, he'd add one more criteria— *doesn't make the roof of my mouth tingle*. It was Carmen all over again, but worse, because he was no longer a lovesick seventeen-year-old and Daniella was his wife. No woman could be allowed to set him on the same catastrophic path as his father, not when Leo knew how hard it was to repurpose himself. What painful test of his inherent all-in personality had he inadvertently set himself up for now?

His marriage was supposed to be about compatibility and convenience, not a headlong sprint into the depths of craziness. It was important to start it off on the right foot.

"Did my driver get all of your belongings?" he asked her and winced.

That wasn't the right foot. *My driver.* As if he regularly employed servants to do his bidding. Was he *really* going to act that pretentious around his new bride? He usually drove himself, for crying out loud. He'd only hired a car because he thought Daniella might enjoy it.

She nodded, taking it in stride. "Yes, thank you."

"Have you said your goodbyes to everyone?"

"Yes. I'm ready."

The conversation was almost painful. This was why he'd rather have a root canal than take a woman to dinner, why he'd opted to skip dating entirely. They were married, well matched and should be able to shoot right past small talk.

Leo waited until they were seated in the town car before speaking again. She crossed her long legs, arranging them gracefully, skin sliding against skin, heels to one side. And he was openly watching her as if it was his own private movie.

Before he started drooling, he peeled his gaze from the smooth expanse of leg below her skirt. "If you don't mind, I'd like to invite my parents over tonight to meet you."

"I would be very happy to meet your parents." She clasped her hands together, resting them in her lap serenely. "You could have invited them to the ceremony. I recall from your profile how important family is to you."

He shrugged, mystified why it pleased him so much that she remembered. "They're less than thrilled about this marriage. My mother would have preferred I marry someone I was in love with."

"I'm sorry." Her hand rested on his sleeve for a brief, reassuring moment, then was gone. "You have to live your life according to what makes sense for you, not your mother."

Everything about her was gracious. Her speech, her mannerisms. Class and style delineated her from the masses and it was hard to believe she'd come from the same type of downtrodden, poverty-stricken neighborhood as he had. She had strength and compassion to spare, and he admired her pledge to care for her mother.

So she possessed a compelling sensuality and he couldn't take his eyes off of her. This was all new. By tomorrow, the edge would surely have worn off.

He relaxed. Slightly.

This marriage was going to work, allowing him to focus on his company guilt-free, while his wife handled wifely things and required none of his attention. He'd paid Ms. Arundel a sizable chunk of change to ensure it.

"Daniella, I realize we barely know each other, but I'd

like to change that. First and foremost, you can always talk to me. Tell me if you need something or have problems. Any problem at all."

"Thank you. That's very kind."

Gratitude beamed from her expression and it made him vaguely uncomfortable, as if he was the lord of the manor, bestowing favors upon the adoring masses. They were equals in this marriage. "As I told you on the phone, I have a lot of social obligations. I'll depend on you to handle them, but you can come to me if you need help or have questions."

"Yes, I understand." She started to say something else and appeared to change her mind, as if afraid to say too much. Probably nervous and unsure.

"Daniella." Leo paused, weighing the best approach to ease the tautness between them. She gazed at him expectantly, her almond-colored eyes bright, with a hint of vulnerability. That nearly undid him. "We're married. I want you to trust me, to feel relaxed around me."

A building was only as good as its foundation.

"I do." She nodded, her expression so serious, he almost told her a joke to see if she'd smile. "You're everything I expected. I'm very happy with Elise's choice."

She was clutching her hands together so tightly, her knuckles had gone white. The art of small talk was not his forte, but surely he could do better than this.

"I'm pleased, as well." Pleased, not happy. This marriage had never been about being happy, but being sensible. "But now we have to live together and it should be comfortable for us both. You can talk to me about anything. Finances. Religion. Politics."

Sex.

His mind had *not* jumped straight to that...but it had, and unashamedly so, with vivid mental images of what her legs looked like under that prim skirt. She glanced at him, held his gaze. A spark flared between them and again, he sensed her energy, coiled and ready to whip out—and his body strained to catch it.

Stop, he commanded his active imagination. He and Daniella had an agreement. A civilized, rational agreement, which did not include sliding a hand over her thigh. His fingers curled and he shoved them under his leg.

She looked down and shifted, angling slightly away. One finger drummed nervously against her skirt. "Thank you. I appreciate that."

His very carnal reaction to a mere glance had obviously upset her.

He cleared his throat. "Are you still okay with letting the intimate side of our relationship unfold naturally?"

Her eyes widened and he almost groaned.

What a fantastic way to set her at ease. He needed to dunk his head in a bucket of cold water or something before he scared her into complete silence. Though that might be better than her constantly starting sentences with *yes,* as if she thought he expected a trained parrot.

"Yes." She met his gaze squarely and earned a couple of points for courage. "Why wouldn't I be?"

Because you feel this draw between us and it's making your palms sweat, too.

Chemistry had been far down the priority list, for both of them.

He just hadn't anticipated having so much of it right out of the gate. Or that it would pose a very real danger of becoming such a distraction, the exact opposite of his intent in hiring a matchmaker.

His focus should be on work. Not on getting his wife naked. Indulgent pleasures weren't on the menu, particularly not for someone with his inability to stop indulging.

"I want to be sure we're on the same page," he said.

"We are. Our marriage will be companionable with a progression toward intimacy when it seems appropriate." Her tone wavered, just a touch, and was coupled with a glint in her eyes he couldn't interpret. "Like we discussed."

His exact words. And suddenly he wished he could take it all back. Wished he could put a glint of happiness in her eyes instead of the look currently drilling a hole through his chest. The unsettling feeling bothered him more than the chemistry, because he had no clue what to do with it.

"We'll have separate bedrooms, for now." That had been his intent from the beginning and seemed even more necessary given her nervousness. It should solve everything. The back of his throat burned with inexplicable disappointment. "Take things slowly."

Separate bedrooms would serve to put some distance between them. Ease the tension, give them both time to acclimate. Give the chemistry time to cool. And definitely allow him to refocus.

Then they'd settle into what he'd envisioned: a marriage where they had fulfilling lives outside of each other and enjoyed a pleasant relationship both in the bedroom and out. No one with his intense personality could have any other kind of marriage.

His phone beeped and he glanced at it. He'd taken a half day to attend his wedding and given his employees the rest of the day off as well, but he was never "out of the office."

The email was a brief courtesy notice from Tommy Garrett's people to let him know Garrett Engineering had narrowed the field to Leo and another firm, Moreno Partners. Excellent. The timing couldn't be better. His new wife could organize the wine and dine for Garrett as soon as she was settled.

"Do you need to make a call?" Daniella asked politely. "I don't mind. Pretend I'm not here."

That wasn't even possible. "Thanks, but it was an email. No response needed."

A different strategy was in order. In light of the wife he'd ended up with, thinking of her as an employee might work best to stave off the urge to spend the weekend in bed, making his wife laugh and then making her gasp with pleasure. And then hitting *repeat* a hundred times.

If he fit Daniella into a predefined box, she'd slide into his life with little disruption and that was exactly what he wanted. What he needed.

Success guaranteed security. It was the only thing that could and no price was too high to ensure he kept his focus on Reynolds Capital Management—even continued solitude.

Dannie kept her mouth shut for the rest of the ride to her new life.

Where she would not share a bedroom with her husband.

She was alternately very glad for the space and very confused. The flash of awareness between them must be one-sided. Or she'd imagined it. Leo could not have been more clear about his lack of interest in her.

Maybe he'd seen right through Elise's makeover.

And now her fantasy about the way he'd kiss if he really meant it had shattered. Such a shame. Her husband was attractive in that unattainable way of movie stars, but in her imagination, he kissed like a pirate on shore leave, and no one could take that away.

She stole a peek at this hard-to-read man she'd married for life.

Her lungs froze. What if Leo decided he didn't like her after all? Just because he claimed to have a strong sense of commitment didn't mean he'd tolerate screwups. And screwups were her specialty.

Her mother was counting on her. She was counting on herself, too. If Leo divorced her, she'd have nothing. One of his first acts upon learning she'd accepted his proposal was to hire a full-time caregiver for her mother who specialized in pulmonary rehabilitation. The nurse was slated to start today.

Without Leo, her mother would surely die a very slow and painful death. And Dannie would be forced to watch helplessly.

Her nails bit into her palm and she nearly yelped. Long nails. Yet another thing she had to get used to, along with all the other things Elise had done to make her over into Leo's perfect wife. Organization and conversation skills came naturally, but the polish—that had taken a while to achieve.

She had to remember her job here was to become the behind-the-scenes support for a successful man. Not to be swept away in a haze of passion for her new husband.

"We're here," Leo said in his smooth voice.

Dannie glanced out the window and tried not to gape. Leo's house practically needed its own zip code.

They'd discussed her comfort level with managing a large house. During the conversation, she'd pictured a two-story, four-bedroom house with a big backyard, located in a quiet suburban neighborhood. That would have been her idea of large after the small two-bedroom apartment she'd shared with her mother.

She'd known the house was in Preston Hollow, one of the most elite neighborhoods of Dallas. But *this* she could never have anticipated.

Wrought-iron gates caught between two large brick-and-stone posts swung open as if by magic and the driver turned the car onto the cobblestone drive leading up to the house. Colossal trees lined the drive, partially blocking the sun and lending a hushed, otherworldly feel to the grounds. And *grounds* was the only fitting term. Neatly manicured grass stretched away on both sides of the car all the way to the high stone wall surrounding Leo's house.

Her house. *Their* house.

The car halted in a semicircular crushed-stone driveway, and the hulking residence immediately cast it in shadow. The manor sprawled across the property, pointy rooflines dominating the brick-and-stone structure. Four—no, five—chimneys stabbed toward the sky.

She should have asked for a picture before agreeing to handle a property this size. What was she *doing* here?

"What do you think?" Leo asked, but it was hardly a question she could answer honestly.

"It's very…" *Gothic.* "Nice."

She bit the inside of her lip. All of Elise's hard work would go up in smoke if Dannie couldn't keep her smart-aleck gene under control. The thought of Elise calmed her. They'd done exhaustive work together to prep Dannie for this, with endless days of learning to set a table, to make proper tea. Practicing how to sit, how to walk, how to introduce people. In between, Elise had transformed Dannie's appearance into something worthy of a magazine cover.

This was it—the test of whether the makeover would stick or Dannie would fail.

With a deep breath, Dannie smiled. "It's beautiful, Leo. I'm very eager to learn my way around."

"Let me show you." He placed a hand at the small of her back as she exited the car and kept it there, guiding and supporting, as they ascended the stone steps to the front door. "Please think of this as your home. Anything you want to change is open for discussion."

Anything. Except the arranged-marriage part.

It was ridiculous to even think that. But her wedding day felt so anticlimactic. And disappointing. She shouldn't be wishing Leo would sweep her up in his arms and carry her over the threshold, Rhett-style. Or wishing they had a timeless romance.

The palm at her back signaled security. Not passion. A partnership based on mutual affection was enough. Dannie was Leo's wife, not the love of his life, and she didn't have the luxury of entertaining daydreams of eventually being both.

Leo led her into the foyer. The interior of the house

opened before her, with soaring ceilings, twenty-foot windows and grand arches leading to long hallways. It reminded her of a cathedral, beautiful and opulent.

The tour of her new home took close to thirty minutes. By the time Leo concluded it in the kitchen, she was out of breath and ready to get started on the first thing she wanted to change—her shoes. The house had *four* flights of stairs.

Leo leaned a hip against the granite island in the center of the kitchen and picked up a cell phone from the counter. "For you. The number is written here, along with the alarm system security codes and the code for wireless internet access."

She took the phone with numb fingers and stared at the glossy screen. Her current cell phone was of the make-a-call-only variety. It would take hours to figure out how this one worked. "Thank you. Is your phone number written down, too?"

"I programmed it into your phone. Here's the user manual." He slid it across the counter and stuck a hand in his pocket, casually, as though they were a normal married couple chatting in the kitchen. "This model has great planning features. Feel free to add things to my schedule as needed. My admin's phone number is programmed in, as well. Mrs. Gordon. She's eager to meet you."

He had an admin, one who knew him far better than Dannie did, like how to make his coffee and whether he paced while on the phone or sat at his desk.

Suddenly, she felt completely out of her depth. "Oh. All right. I'll contact her right away."

"The car and driver will be on call for as long as you like," he continued, and his mellow voice soothed her nerves as he ticked off the items on his mental list. His confidence and self-assurance were potent. "But please, take some time to visit a dealership and buy yourself a car. Whatever kind you like. You'll want the independence."

A *car*. Any car she wanted. She'd been hopping public

transportation for so long, she nearly swooned at the idea. Was there anything he hadn't thought of? "That's very nice. Thank you."

But he wasn't finished waving his benevolence around. "I opened a bank account for you. It will be replenished regularly, but if you find yourself low, let me know. Spend it like it's your money, not mine." From his pocket, he produced a shiny black credit card and handed it to her. "No limit."

"Leo." He'd spun her around so many times now, she could hardly keep her balance. The phone and credit card in her hands blurred as she blinked back overwhelmed, appreciative tears. "This is all very generous. I'm sorry if this is too forward, but I have to ask. Why would you do all this and expect nothing in return?"

His dark eyebrows drew together in confusion. "I expect quite a bit in return, actually."

"I meant in the bedroom."

Leo went still.

Yeah, far too forward. But jeez, really? A no-limit credit card and he didn't even want one conjugal visit a month? There was a punch line here she didn't get and she'd prefer not to have it smack her in the face later.

"Daniella…" Leo swallowed and she realized he was at a loss for words.

Why couldn't she keep her big mouth closed? She should have stuck to *yes* and *thank you*.

"I'm sorry," she said in a rush. "Forgive me. You've been nothing but kind and I have no right to question your motives."

The lines of his handsome face smoothed out and he held up a hand. "No apology needed. I want to have a good relationship, where you feel like we're equals. The best way to achieve that is to give you your own money and the power to do as you like with it."

She stared at him. *Power.* He'd been granting her power with these gestures. The man she'd married was thoughtful, generous and very insightful. This whole experience could have gone very differently. Gratitude welled in her chest. "I don't know what to say."

"You don't have to say anything." He smiled and it was as powerful as it was comforting. "Remember, I'm going to be at the office a lot. You should find a hobby or volunteer work to keep you busy. A car will come in handy."

Implausibly, he was giving her the ability to entertain herself, when her sole focus should be on him and his needs. "Won't I be busy with all your social obligations?"

He waved it off. "That won't take one hundred percent of your time. You're building a life here and when our paths cross, we should enjoy each other's company. You can regale me with stories of the things you're involved in."

Elise had coached her on this extensively. It was part of her role to provide stimulating conversation for Leo's business associates. Who better to practice with than her husband? After all, they *were* a married couple having a chat in the kitchen. "That makes sense."

"Good." His eyes warmed, transforming him from movie-star handsome into something else entirely. Her breath caught.

If that's what happened to his eyes when he was pleased, she *really* wanted to see them stormy with desire.

She shook her head. They were talking about *hobbies*.

Leo took her hand, casually, as if he'd done it a thousand times. "I don't want you to be disappointed by our marriage. In the past, it's been a struggle to balance work and a relationship because the expectations weren't clear from the beginning. Women in my circles tend to demand attention I can't give them and I'm grateful we won't have that issue."

The feel of her hand in his sparked all the way up her arm, unsettling her. It was the only plausible excuse for why she blurted out, "You couldn't find one woman besides me who was willing to forgive your absence in exchange for a life of luxury?"

Her mother would have a coronary if she could hear Dannie being so outspoken. But he'd said in the car they could discuss anything. She hoped he meant it.

"Sure. But I wanted the right woman."

All at once, the reason he'd gone to a matchmaker seemed painfully obvious. He'd tried to buy his way out of putting any effort into a relationship and his previous girlfriends had told him to take a hike. So to avoid a repetition, he bought a wife.

Her.

No wonder he'd been so adamant about honoring commitments. He didn't want her to bail when she figured out she'd be all alone in this big house from now on.

Gothic indeed.

"I see."

"Daniella." His gaze bored into hers, pleading with her to believe…something. But what? "Neither of us have any illusions about this marriage, and that's why it will work. I understand the drive for security. I'm happy to provide it for you because it's a drive we share."

She nodded and excused herself to unpack—and get some breathing room. Security *was* important and she'd married a good, solid man who'd never leave her like her father had. She just hadn't expected gratefulness for that security to blossom into unexpected warmth toward the husband who'd provided it. And who promised to never be around.

As she climbed the stairs to her room, she realized what his unspoken plea had been meant to communicate.

He needed her as much as she needed him.

Three

The scraps of silk had definitely not been in Dannie's suitcase when she packed it.

She fingered the baby-doll lingerie set and noticed the note: "For a red-hot wedding night. —Elise."

Dannie held up the top. Such as it was. Black lace cups overlaid red silk triangles, which tied around the neck halter-style. Red silk draped from the bust, allowing a flirty peek at the tiny G-string panties beneath. Or it would if she was insane enough to actually wear something so blatantly sexy for her husband.

This lingerie was definitely the ticket to a red-hot wedding night. For some other woman, not Daniella Reynolds. Dannie had married a workaholic. With her eyes wide-open.

She tucked the sexy lingerie into the very back of the drawer she'd designated for sleepwear. Ha. There'd be no sleeping going on if she wore *that* outfit. She sighed. Well, it would be the case if her husband pried his eyes off his bottom line. And was attracted to her. And they shared a bedroom.

And what exactly had she expected? That Leo would take one look at his new wife and fall madly in love? She needed to get over herself and stop acting as though Leo had taken away something that she'd never planned on having in the first place.

Elise, the eternal optimist despite being perfectly aware Dannie and Leo had only met that same day, couldn't have known how things would shake out. It was still depressing to be so soundly rejected. How would there be a possibility of children if they didn't share a bedroom?

Dannie slammed the drawer a little harder than an adult probably should have and stomped to the bed to finish unpacking her meager wardrobe.

If she was going to be alone, this was certainly the place to do it. Her bedroom rivaled the finest luxury suite she'd ever seen featured in a movie. She didn't have to leave. Ever. There was a minibar with a small refrigerator, fully stocked. An electronic tablet lay on the bedside table and she suspected Leo had already downloaded hundreds of books since her profile had said she liked to read.

The entertainment center came equipped with a fifty-inch flat-screen TV, cable, a DVD player, a sound system worthy of a nightclub and a fancy touch-screen remote. The owners' manuals lay on the raw silk comforter. Of course. Leo never missed a trick.

She wondered where he kept the owner's manual for Leo Reynolds. That was something she'd gladly read from cover to cover. A forty-seven-point profile only went so far into understanding the man.

There had to be more to Leo than met the eye, because no one voluntarily cut themselves off from people without a reason.

By the time she folded the last pair of socks, the hour had grown late. Leo's parents were due in thirty minutes. She called her mother to see how she was getting along with the nurse and smiled at the effusive recounting of how her mother's new caregiver played a serious game of gin rummy. Her mother sounded happy.

Relieved, Dannie went into the bathroom, where she had left half a cosmetic counter's inventory strewn across the marble vanity. She took a few minutes to organize it in the drawers, which had built-in compartments of different sizes. The bathroom alone was bigger than her entire apartment.

Dannie agonized over what to wear and finally selected a simple pale lavender skirt and dove-gray button-up shirt. Her small wardrobe of coordinated pieces had been another gift from Elise. She was between sizes so everything had to be altered, adding yet more cost to the already expensive clothes. Shoes, however, posed no problems whatsoever. She stepped into a pair of calfskin sling backs that fit as if they'd been custom-made for her foot, then redid her chignon and makeup.

Who *was* that woman in the mirror?

"Daniella Reynolds," she whispered to her reflection, then said it louder to get used to the sound of it. Only telemarketers and her grandmother called her Daniella. She liked the way Leo said it, though.

Since it was far past time to assume her duties as hostess to Leo's parents, she navigated downstairs with only one wrong turn.

Leo was not in the lavishly appointed living room. Or the kitchen, or any of the other maze of rooms on the first floor. Finally she spied his dark head bent over the desk in his study, where he was clearly engrossed in the dollar signs marching across his laptop screen.

Leo was working. Gee. What a shock. Why hadn't she thought to check his study first? Wishful thinking?

For a moment, she watched him, curious to see her husband unguarded. Towering bookshelves lined the room and should have dwarfed the man in it. They didn't. Leo's persona dominated the room. He'd shed his suit jacket and rolled up his shirtsleeves to midforearm. With his hair slightly rumpled, he was kind of adorable.

He glanced up with a distracted, lopsided half smile and her stomach flipped with a long, feminine pull. Okay, he was more than adorable. He was quite delicious and thoroughly untouchable, a combination she suddenly found irresistible. Her inner Scarlett conjured up a naughty mental scenario involving that red-hot lingerie and Leo's desk. *Hey, here's a bottom line you can check out.*

"Busy?" she croaked and cleared her throat. Duh. Of course he was.

"I'm, uh, just finishing up." He shot a furtive glance at his laptop as if the screen contained something shamefully un-work-related.

"What are you doing? Watching YouTube videos?" *Shut up, Scarlett.* It was none of her business whether he was monitoring stock prices or carousing in a role-playing-game forum. "I mean…"

Well, there was really no recovery for that slip.

"No." He shut the lid and she thought that would be the end of it. But then his mouth twitched. "I mentor college students online. I was walking through a business plan with one. Via chat."

"That's wonderful." What in the world was shameful about that? "They must really pay close attention when they see your name pop up. That's like winning the mentor lottery."

Her new husband was so generous and kind. Of course he was. Elise wouldn't have matched her with this man otherwise.

"I mentor anonymously."

"Oh. Why?"

"The business world is—" Flustered, he threaded fingers through his already slightly rumpled hair and she itched to smooth it back for him. "Let's just say my competitors won't hesitate to pounce on weakness. I don't present them with any."

Mentoring the next generation of businessmen could be perceived as a weakness? "Richard Branson mentors young kids. I don't see why he can do it, but you can't."

"He's considered successful." The unspoken *I'm not* hung in the air, but Leo stood and rolled his sleeves down, then rounded the desk, clearly signaling the end of the conversation. "Shall we?"

Her mouth fell open and she clamped it closed, swallowing the dozens of questions that sprang to her lips. His expression had closed off and even she could read the tread-with-caution sign. "Of course."

The doorbell rang and she trailed Leo to the foyer to meet Mr. and Mrs. Reynolds. Leo introduced his parents and Dannie shook hands with smiling, silver-haired Mr. Reynolds.

The spritely woman with Leo's dark hair bounded into the house and swept Dannie up in a fierce hug. "I'm so happy to meet you!"

"I'm happy to meet you, too, Mrs. Reynolds." Dannie breathed in her new mother-in-law's perfume, which reminded her of vanilla cookies.

"Oh, please. I'm Susan."

"I'm sorry, but I was expecting someone…" *Cold. Unforgiving. Judgmental.* "…older."

Susan laughed. "Aren't you sweet? Come with me to the kitchen and let Leo talk to his father while we fetch drinks."

After a glance at Leo to gauge the appropriateness, Dannie followed Susan into the kitchen and proceeded to watch while Leo's mother bustled around gathering glasses and chattering as if they were old friends. Obviously Susan felt comfortable in her son's house. Unlike her son's wife. Dannie wouldn't have known which cabinet contained glasses.

"I apologize for missing the ceremony, Daniella." Susan handed her a glass of tea and touched her shoulder. "It was a stupid, useless protest. But I'm mad at Leo, not you."

"Oh." She had to find a new response. That one was wearing thin. But it had been so appropriate. All day.

"He's just so…*Leo.* You know?" Susan sighed dramatically and Dannie nodded, though she didn't know. But she'd like to. "Too focused. Too intense. Too everything but what matters."

No way was she letting that pass. "What matters?"

"Life. Love. Grandchildren." With narrow eyes, Susan peered at Dannie. "Did he tell you that he draws?"

The tea she'd just sipped almost went down the wrong pipe. "Draws what?"

Susan snorted. "That's what I thought. Leo would rather die than let anyone know he does something frivolous. He can draw anything. Animals. Landscapes. Bridges and buildings. He's very talented. Like his namesake."

"Leo was named after someone who draws?" She envisioned a stooped grandfather doodling cartoon characters on the back of a grocery list.

"Leonardo da Vinci."

Dannie nearly dropped her tea. Leo's full name was Leonardo? Not Leonard? She'd noticed the little extra squiggle at the end of his name on the marriage license but had been so fixated on signing her own name she hadn't thought anything of it.

It shouldn't matter. But it did.

She'd married a man with a romantic name who created art from nothing more than pen and paper. She wanted to see something he'd drawn. Better yet, she wanted him to voluntarily show it to her. To share a deep-seated piece of himself. To connect with his wife.

Leo's mother had torn open a tiny corner of her son's personality and it whipped up a fervor to tear away more. They'd been *matched* and Dannie hungered to learn what they might share beyond a love of books, family and commitment.

"Daniella." Susan crooked her finger and Dannie leaned in. "I get that your marriage to my son is some kind of arrangement and presumably, that's all right with you. I won't pry. But Leo needs someone to love him, someone he can love in return, and neither will come easy. If it's not going to be you, please step aside."

Her pulse hammered in her throat. This marriage was

nothing more than a means to an end. An arrangement between two people based on compatibility, not love—exactly what she'd signed up for. But nothing close to what she wanted, what she dreamed could be possible.

Leo had asked for a wife to run his household, organize his parties and charm his business associates. Most important, his wife should give him what he needed, which wasn't necessarily the same as what he *professed* to need.

The woman behind the man had to be smart about how best to do her job.

Her inner Scarlett snickered and said *new plan.*

"What if it *is* going to be me?"

Leo had such a generous heart, but he cut himself off from people. He needed Dannie's help to understand why. If she could figure him out, it could lead to so much more than an arrangement. It could lead to the enduring love story she'd dreamed of.

Susan's smile could have powered every light in Paris. "Then I say welcome to the family."

Leo shut the door behind his parents and paused a moment before turning. For fortification. It did nothing to ease the screaming awareness of his vibrant wife. Sure enough, when he spun, there she was. Watching him with those keen eyes, chest rising and falling slightly, straining against her soft gray shirt.

He was noticing the way she *breathed.*

Clearly, he needed to go bury himself in a spreadsheet for a couple of hours.

His parents had liked Daniella, fortunately, because their lively discussion covered the fact that Leo hadn't contributed much. He'd been too busy pretending not to be preoccupied by his wife. But she'd been so amazing. A good conversationalist. A good hostess. Warm, friendly. Sexy.

It was just the two of them now. Talking was unavoidable.

"Thank you for entertaining my parents."

She shot him a perplexed look. "You're welcome. That's what I'm here for. Right?"

Since she was gazing at him expectantly, he answered her, though the question should have been rhetorical. "Yes, and I appreciate it."

"I enjoyed meeting your parents. Your mother is very interesting."

That sounded like a lead-up if he'd ever heard one. "What did she say to you in the kitchen?"

"Nothing of consequence." The smile on his wife's face was gracious and innocent. Too much so.

"Don't listen to anything my mother says, Daniella. She suffers from a terrible affliction with no cure—overt romanticism."

"Dannie."

"What?"

She'd inched forward until they were breathing the same air. And her chest nearly touched his with each small inhalation. "Daniella is too formal and stuck-up, don't you think? Call me Dannie."

He shook his head. The more formality the better for his peace of mind. "There's nothing wrong with the name *Daniella*. It's unusual. Beautiful. It suits you."

Her eyes lit up and suddenly, she was the only one breathing because all the organs in his chest stopped functioning. Nothing to the south suffered from the same problem. Everything there hummed on high alert.

"You think I'm beautiful?"

Had he said that? His brain was not refreshing fast enough. "Your name. I said your name is beautiful." Her expression fell and he cursed. If only he could converse with his wife exclusively by email, then maybe he could avoid hurting her feelings. "Of course you are, too. Very lovely."

Nice save, he thought sarcastically. *Lovely.* That described a winter snowscape. From the perspective of an eighty-year-old woman. This was the point where he usually escaped to go do something where he possessed proficiency—work.

Without looking at her again, he muttered, "Good night."

"Leo." A firm hand on his arm stopped him before he'd taken two steps past her. "I asked you to call me Dannie because that's what my friends call me. We're friends, aren't we?"

The warmth in her voice washed over him, settling inside with a slow burn. He didn't turn, didn't dare face her.

Something fundamental had changed in her demeanor—the leash she'd kept on her energy had snapped and yeah, he needed to look out. It leached into the air, electrifying it. She certainly wasn't afraid to speak to him any longer. "I... Yes. Of course."

She brushed against his arm as she rounded it, apparently not content to talk to his back. Her shirt gaped slightly, revealing a tantalizing peek at her cleavage. The slow burn blazed faster. They were talking about being friends, not lovers. What was wrong with him?

Dannie. No, too intimate. *Daniella* was too intriguing. What was he supposed to call her, *hey, you?*

He couldn't compartmentalize his wife. That was bad.

"Friends," he rasped because he had to say something.

Okay, good. Daniella could go into the friends box. It could work. He'd envisioned having a companion to fill a hole in his life. Now he had one.

"Friends." Without breaking eye contact, she reached up and loosened his tie, leaning into it, fingers lingering far too long for the simple task. "Who help each other relax."

Relax? Every nerve in his body skated along a razor's edge, desperately seeking release from the power of his wife's touch. The faint scent of strawberries wafted from her glossy lips and he wanted to taste it. "What makes you think I need to relax?"

"I can feel the tension from here, Leo."

Was that what they were calling it these days? Felt like a good, old-fashioned hard-on to him.

As if pulled by imperceptible threads, his body circled closer to hers and the promise of heat turned into a reality as their lower halves brushed once, twice. His hand flew to the small of her back to clamp her tight against him.

Fingers still tangled in his loosened tie, she tugged slightly. Her face tipped up, lips primed to be taken in another kiss, but this time nothing prevented him from finishing it. From dragging his lips down the length of his wife's torso, straight to…

He cursed—they'd agreed to be platonic only a few hours ago and they were in the middle of an innocuous conversation about being *friends*. Yet he was salivating at the thought of kissing her, of laughing together over a joke, of being so much more than a convenience to each other.

He took a deliberate step backward and her hand dropped from his tie.

If she had this strong an effect on him, he was in hotter water than he'd realized. He did *not* want to be so obsessed with his wife.

"I'm tense because I have a lot of work to do." He willed his body and his bothersome loneliness back into submission. Or tried to. Seemed as though it was destined to be a losing battle. Since she was clearly no longer too scared to talk, he'd have to put space between them another way. "We'll spend time together, but this will not be a conventional relationship. If that's not going to work for you, we should get an annulment."

A hint of hurt crept into her expression. His chest panged. She'd just asked to be friends and loosened his tie. Why was he turning it into a cardinal offense? Wasn't this part of letting their relationship grow more intimate naturally?

"What happened to make you so jaded?" she asked quietly, not the slightest bit cowed by his speech. He liked it better when she said nothing more than *yes* and *thank you*.

"I'm not jaded. I don't have anything against relationships or love in general. Without it, I wouldn't be here. My parents still make googly eyes at each other across the table. Didn't you notice?"

"Of course. They're a very happy couple. Why don't you want the same?"

There was the reason he'd nipped the tie loosening in the bud. They were married and might even become friends, but they were never going to be anything more, and it was a disservice to Daniella to let her have the smallest hope otherwise.

He was already doing himself a disservice by even contemplating "otherwise."

"Oh, they're happy, all right." He rolled his eyes. "At the expense of everything else. My parents have no money. No savings."

And they refused to accept what they called handouts from Leo. He'd like nothing more than to take care of them, had offered a house, cars, even vacations, to no avail. Apparently, they enjoyed the gangs and graffiti spray-painted on the front sidewalk. Their memories appeared to be short, but Leo could never forget the gun-wielding thief who'd broken into their house when he was six. The terror had fueled his drive to escape and kept him on the straight and narrow.

"You fault your parents for being happy over making money?"

"No, I don't blame my father for working a low-paying job so he could be home with my mom and me. I choose to live my life differently. I'll never force my child to be grateful for one gift under the Christmas tree. To stay home from school on the days when the rest of the class goes on field trips to the zoo because I can't afford for my kid to go."

"Oh, Leo."

The compassion shining in her eyes unearthed something poignant inside. That had to go. This wasn't about feeling sorry for poor, little Leo Reynolds from the section of east

Dallas where even the churches had bars on the windows. It was about making a point.

"See all this?" He cut a hand through the air to indicate the house at large. "I worked for every dime. I held three jobs in college so I could graduate with no debt and then put my nose to the grindstone for years to get ahead. I'm still not there. If I take my eye off the prize for even a moment, poof. It all vanishes."

His wife gazed at him without speaking, lips pursed in a plump bow. Firm breasts strained against her blouse, inviting him to spread the fabric wide and—maybe he needed to internalize which prize he wasn't supposed to take his eyes off of.

Other venture capital companies were unearthing the next Google or staking start-ups that sold to competitors for billions of dollars. Reynolds Capital would be there soon if he kept on course. All he had to do was resist temptation. He'd married a woman who would help him avoid the dangers of giving in.

If she'd just stay in her box, that is.

He breathed in the scent of strawberries and the sizzling energy of his wife. "I work, Daniella. All the time. I can't invest in a relationship. It wouldn't be fair if I let you believe in that possibility."

He couldn't let himself dwell on the possibilities, either. No weakness. Indulgence led to immersion and immersion led to ruin. Carmen had proved that, nearly derailing his entire senior year and subsequently, his life. It was easier to never start down that path and the last thing he wanted was to hurt Daniella.

Four

Dannie slept poorly that night. The bed was comfortable, but she wasn't. Leo had her tied up in knots.

Now that she knew how truly earthshaking his eyes looked when they were hot with passion, she didn't know if she'd ever be comfortable again. The spike of awareness inside—deep, *deep* inside—had peaked the second he touched her and then died a miserable death during the "I'm a workaholic, deal with it" conversation.

He was definitely attracted to her. And perfectly willing to ignore it in favor of his bottom line. How exactly did he envision them moving past being polite strangers?

Her new plan might need some refining. Just because she and Leo's mother thought he might benefit from a woman's tender affections didn't mean Leo thought that. And if Dannie irritated him any further with unwanted advances, he might seek that annulment on his own. At which point she'd get nothing and she'd let her mother and Elise down. Plus herself.

But as far she was concerned, they were married for life, and she wanted to eventually be friends *and* lovers. Despite Leo's impassioned speech, she really didn't understand why he didn't want that, too.

Hence the sleepless night.

She woke in the morning, groggy but determined to be a better wife to Leo Reynolds than he could ever dream. Rob had wanted a fade-into-the-background woman and she'd messed up. Elise's training had taught her how to beat back that strong-willed inner Scarlett.

Leo was going to get what he'd asked for.

If she addressed his needs—especially the unrealized ones—maybe *that* would lead them into a deeper relationship.

After she dressed and arrived downstairs, one of the maids informed her Leo had already left for the day. Instead of wallowing in disappointment she had no business feeling, she familiarized herself with the kitchen as she toasted bread and scrambled eggs. Tomorrow morning, she'd set an alarm and be up early to make Leo coffee or breakfast or whatever he preferred, which she needed to learn pronto if she hoped to see him in the morning.

Dannie spent the rest of the morning in an endless parade of tasks: learning the ins and outs of a difficult phone that she refused to believe was smarter than she was, memorizing the brands of Leo's clothes, determining how he preferred his closet to be organized, researching the recommended care of all the fabrics. As mistress of the household, it was her responsibility to ensure the servants did their jobs well and correct poor performance as necessary. By lunch, her brain hurt.

And she hadn't even started on Leo's social calendar.

Once she tapped into the wealth of information named Mrs. Gordon, Dannie breathed a little easier. Leo's admin talked for a solid hour and then sent a dozen emails full of links and instructions about the care and feeding of a venture capitalist.

Dannie read everything twice as she absently shoved a sandwich in her mouth.

Mrs. Gordon wrapped up the exchange with a tip about an invitation to an alumni event from Leo's college, which was that very night. She kindly agreed to delete the reminder entry she'd already set up so Dannie could practice scheduling.

Perfect. Dannie plunked the stupid phone into her palm and eyed it. "I'm the boss. You better cooperate," she told it, and proceeded to manhandle the appointment onto Leo's calendar.

When his acceptance appeared, she nearly broke into an impromptu dance. Until she noticed she'd scheduled it for tomorrow night. Grimly, she rescheduled and got it right the second time. Leo was probably sitting in his office shaking his head as he accepted the updated request.

Enough of that job. Dannie went to agonize over her meager wardrobe in anticipation of her first social appearance as Mrs. Leo Reynolds. This she'd have to get right on the first shot. She couldn't carry a second outfit in her clutch in case of dress remorse.

Leo walked through the door at precisely six o'clock. Dannie was ready and waiting for him in the kitchen, the closest room to the detached garage. The salmon-colored dress she wore accentuated her figure but had tasteful, elegant lines. Elise had taught her to pick flattering clothes and it looked fantastic on her, especially coupled with strappy Jimmy Choos heels. Would Leo notice?

"How was your day?" she asked politely while taking in the stress lines and shadows around his eyes that said he'd slept poorly, as well.

Something unfolded in her chest, urging her to smooth back the dark hair from his forehead and lightly massage his temples. Or whatever would soothe him. She wanted to know what to do for him, what he'd appreciate.

He set a brown leather messenger bag on the island in the kitchen. "Fine. And yours?"

"Wonderful." Except for the part where he hadn't kissed her goodbye. Or hello. *Shut up, Scarlett.* "The alumni gala is at the Renaissance Hotel. My driver will take us as soon as we're ready."

He hadn't said a word about her dress. Perhaps she'd take that as a sign he wouldn't be ashamed to be seen with her and not dwell on whether it got a response or not. Compliments weren't the reason she'd married Leo.

"That's fine. Let me change and we'll go." Leo set off for the stairs, fingers already working on his tie, which she'd have gladly taken off for him, if he'd let her. "They're giving an award to a friend of mine, and we should take him to dinner afterward."

Reservations. Where? For how many? But Leo was gone before she could ask.

Totally winging it, she called the most expensive restaurant she'd heard of and booked a table for four in Leo's name. If nothing else, the restaurant might be willing to add a few more to the party for a distinguished guest like Leo Reynolds.

Leo returned to the kitchen a short time later and she forgot all about a little thing like reservations. In black tie, Leo simply stole her breath.

"Ready?" he asked with raised eyebrows, likely because her fish-mouth impersonation amused him.

He was so delicious with his dark hair and dark suit, all crisp and masculine with a slight sensuous edge that set off something sharp and hot inside her. Last night, she'd felt just enough of the body he carried under that suit and the memory reintroduced itself as she let her eyes travel the entire length of her husband.

He cleared his throat and her gaze snapped to his. He was still waiting on her response.

"Ready," she squeaked and grabbed her clutch.

Leo kept up the conversation as they rode to the hotel with his confident, steady presence. She suspected—and appreciated—it was a ploy to dispel her nervousness, but it didn't work.

Leo escorted her through the lobby of the hotel with a hand at the small of her back. She liked the way his hand fit there. It served a dual purpose of providing support and showing everyone they were together.

And boy, did people notice. Heads swiveled as they entered the crush in the Renaissance ballroom. A string quartet played Strauss on a small platform in the corner, but the music couldn't cover the rush of whispers that surely were about the woman with Leo.

One flawless society wife in progress. Who hadn't gone to college but was going to be brilliant or die trying. Dannie squared her shoulders.

The neckline of her dress slipped, revealing a healthy slice of breast. Surreptitiously, she fingered it back into place. The deep vee over her cleavage wasn't terribly daring, but it was low-cut and the spaghetti straps were too long for her torso. Since the svelte salmon-colored dress had cost Elise seven hundred dollars, paying to have it altered felt like a sin.

It slipped down again as Leo steered her toward the far corner. As she walked, she lowered one shoulder, Quasimodo-style, hoping to nudge the neckline back where it belonged through a combination of shifting her balance and sheer will.

"Are you okay?" Leo whispered.

She should have worn the dress all day and practiced walking in it. Hindsight. Double-sided tape could have fixed the problem in a jiffy.

"Of course." She pasted on a serene smile as they halted before a group of men and women Leo clearly knew. Nodding, she greeted people and used all her tricks to remember names. Constantly being fired from a variety of jobs had an upside—few situations or people intimidated her.

"And this is Jenna Crisp," Leo concluded, indicating a gorgeous redhead on the arm of Leo's friend Dax Wakefield, who was receiving the alumni award that evening. "Jenna, this is my wife, Daniella Reynolds."

Dannie shook the woman's hand but Jenna wasn't looking at her. The redhead's attention was on Leo. Hmm. Dannie glanced at him. He didn't notice Jenna's scrutiny. Too busy discussing a patent infringement case with Dax. "I'm happy to meet you, Jenna. Have you known Leo long?"

Jenna focused on Dannie, and her expression noticeably cooled. "Long enough. How did you two meet, again?"

The redhead's tone oozed with challenge, as if there might be something tawdry to the story.

That was one area they'd definitely not covered. Did his friends know he'd gone to a matchmaker? She'd have to settle for a half-truth lest she embarrass Leo. "A mutual acquaintance introduced us."

"Interesting." The other woman nodded, sweeping long locks over her bare shoulders. She curled her lips in a semblance of a smile, which didn't fool Dannie for a second. Jenna did not like her.

"That's how Dax and I met, too. Leo introduced us."

"Oh?" Leo—a matchmaker himself? That *was* interesting. "I'm sure he was happy to help his friends find each other."

"You think so? Considering the fact that Leo and I were dating at the time, I wasn't sure what to make of it."

Oh, dear. No wonder the daggers in Jenna's eyes were so sharp. Dannie groaned inwardly. The dinner reservations had just gotten a whole lot more complicated than whether the table would be big enough.

"I'm sorry. I can't speak for Leo. If you're curious about his motives, you'd best ask him. Champagne?" she offered brightly, intending to put some distance between herself and Leo's ex-girlfriend. At least until she figured out how to navigate the bloody water full of sharks her husband had dropped her into.

"That would be lovely," Jenna said just as brightly and took Leo's arm to join in his conversation with Dax, physically blocking Dannie from the group.

In historical novels, they called that the cut direct. In real life, Dannie called it something else entirely, and if she said that many four-letter words out loud, Leo would have a heart attack.

Instead, she went to get Jenna and Leo a glass of champagne.

Really, she understood Jenna's animosity. She'd be confused, too, if Leo had shuffled her off on a friend and then promptly married someone else. Dannie also had the superior position between them, a point Jenna likely hadn't missed. At the end of the day, Dannie's last name was Reynolds and Jenna's wasn't.

Now she wondered what had really happened between Jenna and Leo. It was a little uncivilized of Leo not to have warned her. Men. Didn't he realize what he'd dragged Dannie into?

In reality, he probably hadn't considered it a problem. And it wasn't. Their marriage was an arrangement and her emotions weren't Leo's primary concern. That put a little steel in her spine. She had a job to do.

When she rejoined the group, Leo shot her a sidelong smile in gratitude for the glass of champagne. The flutters his very private grin set off were enough to forgive him. Almost.

A good wife might choose to forget the whole conversation. She bit her lip.

Then again, a good wife who paid attention to unspoken nuances might also ensure she didn't mistakenly cause her husband embarrassment. Forewarned was forearmed, and if Leo expected her to chat up his associates, she should know exactly what that association was. Right?

"You used to date Jenna?" she murmured in his ear as Dax engaged his date in their own conversation.

"Briefly." Leo's gaze sought out the woman in question, his eyes narrowing and growing a tad frigid. "She told you? I'm surprised she'd be so tactless. And I apologize if I put you in an uncomfortable position."

He'd leaned in, breath teasing along her cheek as he

spoke, and she caught a whiff of something fresh and maybe a little wintry but definitely all male. His hip brushed hers. Heat pooled at the contact and spread, giving a whole new meaning to an uncomfortable position.

She waved off his apology. "Nothing I can't handle. I'm sure you didn't do it on purpose."

He'd apologized instead of calling her out for sticking her nose in his business. That was a relief. Walking that line between being a complement to Leo and fading into the background was harder than she'd anticipated. Regardless, she was going to be a star wife. No compromise.

Leo frowned. "We only went out for a little while and obviously it didn't work out, or I wouldn't have introduced her to a friend. Jenna wanted more than I could give and Dax pays attention to her. It seemed perfect."

Oh. Of course. Jenna was the reason Leo needed a wife who wouldn't expect him to be around—she'd presumed to spend time with a man she liked and grew weary of the "I'm a workaholic, deal with it" speech.

The longing glances Jenna kept throwing Leo's way made a heck of a lot more sense now. Despite most likely being told in no uncertain terms not to get emotionally involved, Jenna had done it anyway. Only to be cast aside.

It was a sobering reminder. Dannie had a lot to lose if she made the same mistake.

Sobering. But ineffective.

As her husband's hand came to rest against the small of her back, she couldn't help but be tremendously encouraged that Leo had cared enough about Jenna to help her find happiness with someone better suited for her. In the kitchen yesterday, he'd expressed genuine interest in ensuring Dannie wasn't disappointed with their marriage.

Small gestures, but in Dannie's mind, they added up to something much larger. He had a good heart underneath all that business acumen. And despite his determination to keep her at arm's length, he needed her to break through the shell he kept around himself.

But how?

The champagne left a bitter taste in Leo's mouth.

If he'd known Jenna would deliberately upset Daniella, he'd never have brought his wife within a mile of her.

He should be having a conversation with Miles Bennett, who was about to launch a software product with some good buzz around it. John Hu was on his radar to speak to as well, and there John was by the bar, talking to Gene Ross's ancient wife. That conversation couldn't be about anything other than Mrs. Ross's show poodle or Miami this time of year, and Leo had no qualms about interrupting either.

Several recent investments hadn't panned out the way he'd hoped. He needed new blood now. Yesterday would have been better.

Instead of the dozen other things he should be doing, he was watching his wife. Out of the corner of his eye, no less, while he pretended to talk to Dax, who pretended he didn't notice Leo's fixation.

Daniella dazzled everyone, despite Jenna's mean-spirited disclosure.

The mechanics of marriage were still new and he hadn't fully considered the potential ramifications of introducing the two women. A wife was supposed to be *less* complicated than regular females, not more. Was Daniella uncomfortable being in the same room with Jenna? Or was she taking it in stride like everything else?

Daniella didn't *look* upset. She looked like a gift-wrapped present he'd put on his list a month ago and Christmas was still a week away.

That dress. It dipped against her breasts, revealing just enough to be interesting but not enough to be labeled indecent. The zipper in the back called his name. One tug and the wrapping would peel away, revealing a very nice gift indeed. The delicate shoes she wore emphasized her shapely legs and he liked that far more than he wanted to.

Daniella was the most gorgeous woman in the room. And the most interesting, the most poised and the most vivacious. Bar none. And he wasn't the only one who thought so, instilling in him a quiet sense of pride with every appreciative glance she earned.

In case she was more upset about Jenna than she let on, he kept a close eye on her as she talked to a couple of Reynolds Capital's partners. No hardship on his part to watch her graceful hands gesture and her pink-stained lips form words. Then she laughed and the dress slipped a tantalizing inch farther down her breasts. And then another inch.

A flash of heat tensed his entire body and tightened his pants uncomfortably.

He swore and Dax stared at him as if he'd lost his mind. Which didn't appear to be as far out of the realm of possibility as it should.

"I need a refill," Leo explained and waved his empty champagne flute at a passing waiter.

When the waiter returned, he downed the glass in two gulps. It didn't cool him down. Something needed to change, very quickly.

He glanced at Daniella. She didn't turn her head, but her eyes swiveled and she met his gaze with a secret smile, as if to say, *later*.

Or maybe that was his lower half projecting her meaning. The upper half refused to entertain even one little fantasy about later. Intimacy was supposed to be a progression, and abandoning that idea on day two didn't bode well for Leo's state of mind.

They hadn't developed a *friendship* yet and he was fantasizing about skipping right over that.

The music swelled, signaling the start of the awards ceremony. Daniella moved toward him at the same moment he stepped forward to grasp her arm. They bumped hips and somehow, the button on his jacket caught her dress.

One of Daniella's nipples popped free of the fabric, searing his vision and sending a surge straight to his groin. She gasped with a feminine squeal of humiliation, hands flying to her chest.

Instantly, Leo whirled her into a snug embrace, hiding her from view. And oh, dear God. His wife's body aligned with his like flowing honey, clinging sweetly to every groove.

"No one saw," he murmured into her hair and prayed she wouldn't take offense to the obvious erection pushing into her abdomen. It wasn't as though he could step away and compose himself.

The sight of that bare, rosy nipple was emblazoned on his brain and worse, both of her nipples pressed against his chest, raising the temperature in the stuffy ballroom about a hundred degrees.

"Are you all...arranged?" he asked hoarsely.

She was shaking. Or was that him?

"I can't," she whispered and her hand worked between their bodies, brushing his erection an ungodly number of times. "The button won't come loose."

He nearly groaned. "We'll have to get to the hall. Somehow. Can you turn?"

"Yes. If you keep your arm around me."

They did a fair impression of Siamese twins, shuffling as one toward the back of the ballroom, Daniella clutching Leo with one hand and her dress with the other. Which meant her hands were nowhere near his erection—and that was good. One more brush of those manicured nails against him would have produced fireworks better left unlit in public.

Miraculously, the crowd had thinned. The awards presenter droned from the next room. Leo was missing the ceremony but Dax would have to understand.

An eternity later, they reached the hall and Leo hustled

Daniella into a deep alcove housing a giant sculpture of a mermaid.

"We're totally hidden from view. It's okay," he said.

She took a half step backward, as far as their tangled clothes would allow.

"My definition of okay and yours must be different." Head bent, she studiously fingered the threads holding his button hostage until they finally came apart. "I'm sorry, Leo. You must be mortified."

Her head was still down, as if she didn't want to look at him.

"Me?" He tipped her chin up with a loosely fisted hand. Her cheeks were on fire. "You're the one who has a reason to be mortified. I can't imagine how you must feel. First I force you to make nice to Jenna and then almost rip off your dress. I'm the one who's sorry."

"It's not *your* fault," she countered fiercely. "This dress doesn't fit quite right. I shouldn't have worn it."

Five minutes ago, he'd have agreed. If she'd dressed a little more matronly, he might be having that conversation with John Hu right now. Except the alternative—being wedged into a secluded alcove with his wife—suddenly didn't seem so terrible. "That dress fits you perfectly."

She shook her head as she twisted the waistline back into place. "All my clothes have to be altered. I know that. But I didn't have this one done. Stupid. I should have thought about the consequences. My job is to make you look good, not embarrass you in public. I'm sorry. I'm not making a very good first impression."

That's what she was worried about? That she'd messed up and displeased him? A weight settled onto his chest. Did she think he was that concerned about their agreement?

Obviously so.

"On the contrary, you've made a great impression. Exactly as I expected. I watched you with my business associates. They liked you." She'd charmed them easily and he could already envision her doing the same at future events. Daniella was amazing, through and through.

"Really?" The disbelief in her voice settled that weight a little deeper. She seemed so disheartened by what was such a small blip in the evening.

Daniella was his wife, not a casual date he might or might not see again. The very act of making her his wife changed everything. He wanted her to be happy, which he hadn't planned, could never have predicted. Not only did he want her to be happy, he'd discovered a healthy drive to care for her and ensure her security. He wanted her to know she could depend on him, always.

Problem being, of course, that his experience with serious relationships started and ended with the woman in front of him.

He nodded, scouting for a way to put a smile back on her face. "If nothing else, you can take solace in the fact that your wardrobe malfunction didn't take place on national TV."

She laughed, as he'd intended. The resurrection of his hard-on, he hadn't. But who could blame him? Her laugh curled through him like fine wine and came coupled with the distinct memory of her beautiful breast.

The secluded alcove grew close and heavy with awareness as she locked on to his gaze. Her irises warmed. "Thank you for rescuing me. It was very chivalrous."

The back of his neck heated at the adoration in her eyes. He felt like a fake. There wasn't a romantic bone in his body. "I wouldn't have abandoned you."

"Your button." Without breaking eye contact, she touched it with her fingertips. "It's loose."

"No problem." He swallowed and his throat was on fire. Everything was on fire. "I have another one."

Slim eyebrows arched as she cocked her head. Loose tendrils of dark brown hair fell against her cheeks and he barely resisted an urge to tuck them back for her. And as a treat for himself. The shiny, slightly wavy locks would be soft against his fingers.

"Should we rejoin the party?" she asked in an incredible show of courage. Not many people would walk back into a room where they'd performed a free peep show. His admiration for her swelled. "As long as I don't move around too much, I should stay tucked away."

His gaze dropped to her cleavage automatically. She was quite tucked away, but the promise of what he knew lay beneath the fabric teased him. How easily he could thumb down that dress and run the pads across those taut nipples. No effort required at all. No one could see them back here behind the sculpture.

He sucked in a hot breath.

"Leo," she murmured and slid lithe fingers along his lapels, straightening them as she traveled south.

"Hmm?" She was so close he could see golden flecks in her eyes. Raw energy radiated from her, wrapping around him in a heated veil.

"The party?" Her lips met on the last syllable and he recalled how they'd sparked against his when he'd kissed her at their wedding ceremony.

This was like a first date, wasn't it? He'd kissed women on dates, lots of times. It might even be considered expected. A major disappointment if he didn't do it.

Would kissing her be as hot the second time? Hotter?

His curiosity would only be satisfied one way.

"We should go back. Shouldn't we?" she asked. But she stood there, frozen, peeking up from beneath her lashes coyly, as if she could read the intent in his eyes.

Yes. They should go back. His body strained toward her, desperate to be closer.

The scent of strawberries wafted to him on a sensuous cloud as she swayed into his space. Or maybe he was the one who moved.

Like honey, he thought as their bodies met. Their lips

touched hesitantly, then firmly, deliberately, and his mind pushed out everything except the sizzle of flesh on flesh.

His wife's mouth opened under his and he swept her deep into his embrace as he kissed her. His back hit the wall but he scarcely noticed as Daniella came alive, hands in his hair, her mouth strong and ferocious against his.

Hunger thundered through his veins. His hips circled against hers involuntarily, uncontrollably as he sought to ease the ache she'd inflamed. With one hand, he enveloped her neck and pushed, tipping her head back so he could open her wider, then tentatively stroked her tongue with his.

She stroked him back, deeper, harder. Leo groaned against her mouth. She kissed like a horny teenager's fantasy. Deep. Wet. Carnal.

Those perfect breasts haunted him. *Touch them,* his libido begged. The temptation was almost too much to bear, but he feared if he gave in to it, he might never surface.

Home. They could go home. Right now. They lived together, after all.

If he took her home, he could strip that dress away to taste every peak and valley of his wife's body. Especially the parts he hadn't yet seen but could feel easily through the silky drape of cloth over her luscious skin.

The kiss deepened, heating further, enflaming his skin. Desire screamed through his body. He'd never kissed a woman on a date quite like this. Hell, he'd never kissed a woman like this *ever,* not even in bed.

She was luring him into a dark pit of need and surfacing suddenly wasn't so appealing.

He trailed openmouthed kisses along her throat and palmed her sexy rear again. Unbelievably, this incredible, stimulating woman was *his.* She moaned under his touch and her head fell back.

"Leo," she murmured as he slipped a pin from her fancy done-up hair. "Don't you need to go back?"

As if she'd thrown a bucket of water over him, his lust-hazed bubble burst. They were in the hallway of a hotel and his wife was reminding *him* of the importance of circulating at the alumni ceremony.

He pulled back to breathe the cool air of sanity. "I do."

Her face remained composed, but a storm of desire brewed in her gaze, one he suspected would easily explode again with his touch. She'd been just as turned on as he had.

"Till later, then?" she asked.

Oh, no. That wouldn't do at all. *Focus, Reynolds.*

At least four people he must speak with mingled in the ballroom less than a hundred yards away and his wife's mussed hair and plump, kiss-stung lips alone threatened to steal his composure. If he had to suffer through the rest of the night while anticipating *later,* nothing of consequence would be accomplished.

You're weak, the nasty voice of his conscience whispered. And that was the real reason he couldn't lose his single-mindedness.

If he let himself indulge—in drawing, in a woman, in *anything* other than the goal—he'd be lost. Look what had just happened with a simple kiss.

He released her and his body cooled a degree or two. It wasn't enough to erase the imprint of her in his senses. "I apologize. That was inappropriate. Please, take a few moments in the ladies' room and meet me back in the ballroom. We'll act as if that never happened."

Disappointment replaced the desire in her expression and made him feel like a world-class jerk.

"If that's what you want."

It was absolutely not what he wanted. But distance was what he needed in order to get a measure of control.

This marriage should be the perfect blend of necessity and convenience. *Should be.* But the possibility of being friends was already out the window due to the curse of his weaknesses, and it would only get worse the further under his skin she dug.

"This is a business event and I haven't been treating it like one."

"Of course." Her tone had become professional, as it should. Even in this, she remained poised, doing her duty as expected, because *she* wasn't weak. She was thoroughly brilliant.

He hated putting up a barrier, but she'd become exactly what he'd suspected she would—a disturbance he couldn't afford.

But she was also proving to be exactly what he'd hoped. The perfect complement of a wife. She deserved happiness and he'd provide no assurance of security—for either of them—if he took his eye off the success of Reynolds Capital Management for even a moment. His wife would not be forced into the poorhouse because of him, like his father had done to Leo's mother.

No more digressions. It was too dangerous to kiss her. Or think about her as a friend.

Daniella was back in the employee box. She had to stay there.

How in the world was he going to forget what those strawberry-scented lips could do?

Five

Leo was already gone by the time Dannie emerged from her bedroom the next morning. Even though she'd set an alarm, he still beat her.

She'd screwed up at the alumni gala. Leo had been kissing her—*oh, my God,* had he been kissing her—and then he hit the brakes. Of course work came first, and the woman behind the man should never forget that. But to pretend *that kiss* hadn't happened? It was impossible. She wasn't naive enough to believe she'd break through his shell in one evening, but she thought she'd lifted it a little at least.

At home, his obsession with work shouldn't be a factor, especially before he left for the office. Tomorrow morning, she'd shove the alarm back thirty minutes. If she beat him to the kitchen, they'd have a chance to talk and maybe share a laugh. Then think about each other fondly over the course of the day.

All good elements of both friendship and marriage.

The next morning she missed him again, and continued to miss him for a week.

Four declined event appointments should have clued her in, but it wasn't until she caught the startled look on his face when he came out of his bedroom one morning that she realized he'd been avoiding her.

"Good morning." She smiled despite his wary expression and the fact that she'd been awake since five hoping to catch him.

"Morning." He nodded and brushed past without another word.

Stung, she watched him retreat down the stairs and vowed not to think about Leo Reynolds the rest of the day. She had a job to do here.

Dannie spent an hour with the staff going over weekly household accounts, then interviewed a prospective maid to replace one who had given notice. She enjoyed organizing Leo's life. At the alumni gala, she'd navigated Leo's social circles, recovered from a humiliating dress fail and smiled through dinner with her husband's ex-girlfriend.

What more could Leo possibly want in a wife?

At four o'clock, Leo texted her with a short message she'd come to expect: I'll be home late. Make dinner plans on your own.

As she'd been doing for a week. Leo clearly planned to keep her at arm's length, despite *that kiss*.

Fuming, she called her mother and invited her over for dinner. Might as well take advantage of the cook Leo kept on staff. She and her mother ate prime rib and lobster bisque, both wonderfully prepared, but neither could keep her attention. Her mother raved about the food, about Dannie's marriage, about how much she liked her new nurse. Dannie smiled but nothing penetrated the cloud of frustration cloaking what should have been a nice evening with her mom.

As far back as Dannie could remember, her mother had constantly passed on relationship advice: *Men don't stick around. Don't listen to their pretty words and promises.* And variations aplenty espousing the evils of falling in love. The whole point of this arranged marriage was so Dannie wouldn't end up alone and miserable like her mother. And despite her mother's best attempts to squash Dannie's romanticism, it was still there, buried underneath reality.

All men couldn't be like her father. Leo didn't flatter her with slick charm, and he'd been nothing but honest with her. Furthermore, her husband had kissed her passionately, madly, more completely than Dannie had ever been kissed in her life. She couldn't pretend it hadn't happened or that she didn't want more than an occasional text message out of her marriage.

They'd never get past being virtual strangers at this rate. Maybe it was for the best, if Jenna's fate bore any credence to what might become Dannie's story. But she couldn't accept that she and Leo would *never* see each other. Surely they could spend a little time together. An hour. Thirty minutes.

How was she supposed to handle his social commitments and take care of his every need if he kept avoiding her?

After she saw her mother off in the chauffeured car that Dannie couldn't quite give up yet, she parked on the couch nearest the stairs, determined to wait for Leo until the cows came home, if necessary. They needed to talk.

An hour later, Dannie started to wonder if Leo intended to sleep at the office. He wouldn't. Would he? Had she screwed up so badly that he couldn't even stand to be in the same house with her?

She flung her head back on a cushion and stared at the ceiling. He certainly hadn't lied to her. He did work all the time and she had done nothing to find her own amusements. Because she didn't want to. She wanted to be Leo's wife in every sense of the word, or at least she thought she did, despite being given little opportunity to find out.

Another hour passed. This was ridiculous. Not only was he hindering her ability to take care of him, but he'd agreed they could be friends. How did he think friendship developed?

New tactics were in order. Before she could remind herself of all the reasons she shouldn't, she sent Leo a text message: I heard a noise. I think someone is in the house. Can you come home?

Immediately, he responded: Call the police and hit the intruder alarm.

She rolled her eyes and texted him back: I'm scared. I'd like you to come home.

Leo: Be there as soon as I can.

Bingo. She huffed out a relieved breath. It had been a gamble, but only a small one. Leo had a good heart, which wouldn't have allowed him to do anything else but come home to his wife.

Twenty minutes later, Leo pulled into the drive at the front of the house. Dannie flicked on the enormous carriage lights flanking the entrance arch, illuminating the wide porch, and met him on the steps.

"Are you okay?" he asked, his hard gaze sweeping the shadows behind her.

His frame bristled with tension, saying in no uncertain terms he'd protect her from any threat imaginable, and it pulled a long, liquid flash from her core that sizzled. An intruder wouldn't stand a chance against so much coiled intensity.

"I'm fine." In a manner of speaking.

Leo's dark suit looked as superb on him as a tuxedo did. More so, because he was at full alert inside it, his body all hard and masculine. Warrior Leo made her mouth water. She might have to fan herself.

"Did you call the police?" He ushered her inside quickly, one hand steady at her back.

"No. I didn't hear the noise again and I didn't want to waste anyone's time." Especially since the noise was entirely fictional. Hopefully, once she hashed things out with Leo, an excuse wouldn't be necessary to get his attention.

He shot off a series of questions and she answered until he was satisfied there was no imminent danger. "Next time, push the panic button. That's what the security alarm is for."

"Did I interrupt something important at work?"

Lines deepened around his eyes as his carriage relaxed and he smiled. "It's all important. But it's okay. It'll still be there in the morning."

Relaxed Leo was nice, too. So much more approachable. She returned his smile and tugged on his arm. "Then sit down for a minute. Tell me about your day."

He didn't budge from his statue impression in the foyer. "Not much to tell. Why don't you go on up to bed? I'll hang out downstairs and make sure there's really nothing to worry about."

Oh, no, you don't. "I'm not tired. You're here. I'm here. Come talk to me for a minute."

He hefted the messenger bag in his hand a little higher in emphasis with an apologetic shrug. "I have some work to finish up."

"That'll be there in the morning, too." Gently, she took the bag from him and laid it on the Hepplewhite table against the wall, a little surprised he'd let her. "We haven't talked since the alumni gala."

The mere mention of it laced the atmosphere with a heaviness that prickled her skin. Leo's gaze fell on hers and silence stretched between them. Was he remembering the kiss? Or was he still determined to forget about it? If so, she'd like to learn that trick.

"There's a reason for that," he finally said.

Her stomach tumbled at his frank admission that he'd been avoiding her. She nodded. "I suspected as much. That's why I want to talk."

His gaze swept over her face. "I thought you wanted me to tell you about my day."

"I do." She started to reach out but stopped as she took in the firm line of his mouth. "But we need to talk regardless. I was hoping to be a little more civil about it, though."

"Maybe we can catch up tomorrow." He picked up the messenger bag from the table, but before he could stride from the foyer, she stepped in front of him, blocking his path.

Arms crossed, she stared him down. "Be straight with

me. I can handle it. Are you regretting your choice in wives? Maybe you're wishing you'd picked Jenna after all?"

The bag slipped from Leo's hand and thunked to the floor. "Not now, Daniella."

"You mean *not now,* and by the way, *not ever?* When will we have this conversation if not now?" Too annoyed to check her action, she poked a finger in his chest. Being demure had gotten her exactly nowhere. "You've been avoiding me. I want to know why. Am I not performing up to your expectations?"

"I'm not avoiding you." Guilt flitted through his expression, contradicting the statement. "I've got three proposals out, the shareholder value on one of my major investments took a forty percent loss over the last week and a start-up I staked declared bankruptcy today. Is that enough truth for you? The reason we haven't talked is because I'm extremely busy keeping my company afloat."

The Monet on the wall opposite her swirled into a mess of colors as she shared some of that guilt. "I'm sorry. I shouldn't have bothered you about the noise. I just wanted to…" *See you. Talk to you. Find out if you've been thinking of me.* "Not be scared."

Leo's expression softened and he reached out to grip her shoulder protectively. "You shouldn't have been. I had the security system installed as soon as you agreed to marry me and it's top-of-the-line. It would take a SWAT team to breach it. You're safe here. Do you not feel like you are?"

She stared up into his worried blue eyes and her insides liquefied. He genuinely cared about the answer. "I do."

It dawned on her then that Leo did a lot behind the scenes—far more than she'd realized. Almost as if he preferred for no one to know about all the wonderful gestures he made or that he was such a kind person underneath. Was he afraid she'd figure out he cared about her more than he let on?

"Good." The worry slipped from his expression and was

replaced with something that looked an awful lot like affection. "The last thing I want is for you to feel anxious or
insecure."

Perfect segue. They shared a drive for security. Surely
he'd understand her need to settle things. "You know what
would make me feel a lot less anxious? If I knew what was
going on between us." Emboldened by the fact that Leo had
cared enough to rush home for her, she went on. "We're supposed to enjoy each other's company when we cross paths,
but we never cross paths."

"We just went out a week ago," he protested with a glint
in his eye that warned her to tread carefully.

She wasn't going to. If Leo pulled another disappearing
act, this might be her only chance to make her case. Besides, he said they could talk about anything.

"Exactly. A whole week ago and we haven't spoken since
then, other than a terse 'Good morning.' I can't handle your
life if I'm not in it. Besides, our relationship won't ever develop without deliberate interaction. On both our parts."

"Daniella." He put a thumb to his temple. Great, now she
was giving him a headache. "What are you asking of me?"

He said it as if she hoped he'd blow through the door and
ravish her, when all she really wanted was a conversation
over a nice glass of wine. "For starters, call me Dannie. I
want to be friends. Don't you?"

Wariness sprang into his stance. "Depends on your definition of friends. The last time you brought that up, I got the
distinct impression it was a euphemism for something else."

"You mean sex?" Oh, Scarlett had just been chomping at
the bit to get in the middle of this conversation, hadn't she?

Leo gave a short nod. "Well, to be blunt."

Oh, no. There was that word again. Her last fight with
Rob flashed through her mind and she swallowed. Was she
trying to ruin everything?

But Leo wasn't a spineless, insecure guy like Rob who

couldn't handle a woman's honest opinion. Besides, this was her marriage and she was prepared to go to the mat for it.

"Our marriage apparently calls for blunt. Since I might not get another opportunity to speak to you this century, here it is, spelled out for you. My offer of friendship is not a veiled invitation to jump me."

His brows rose. "Then what is it?"

Laughter bubbled from her mouth. "Guess I don't spell as well as I think I do. Didn't we decide our relationship would eventually be intimate?" *Not blunt enough.* "Sorry, I mean, that we'd eventually have sex?"

To Leo's credit, he didn't flinch. "We did decide that. I envision it happening very far in the future."

Gee, that made her feel all warm and fuzzy. "Great. Except intimacy is about so much more than shedding clothes, Leo. Did you think we'd wake up one day and just hop into bed? It doesn't work like that. There's an intellectual side to intimacy that evolves through spending time together. By becoming *friends*. I want to know you. Your thoughts. Dreams. Sex starts in here." She tapped her forehead. "At least it does for me."

"You want to be romanced," he said flatly.

"I'm female. The math shouldn't be that hard to do."

"Math is one of my best skills."

What was that supposed to mean? That he'd done the math and knew that's what she wanted—but didn't care? She stumbled back a step.

With her new distance, the colors of the Monet swirled again, turning from a picture of a girl back into a jumble of blotches.

She and Leo needed to get on the same page. She took a deep breath. "How did *you* think we were going to get from point A to point B?"

"I never seemed to have any trouble getting a woman interested before," he grumbled without any real heat. "Usually it's getting them uninterested that's the problem."

Ah, so she'd guessed correctly from the very beginning. "You've never had to invest any energy in a relationship before, have you?"

Gorgeous, well-spoken, rich men probably never did as often as women surely threw themselves at them. He'd probably gone through a series of meaningless encounters with interchangeable women.

"I don't have time for a relationship, Daniella," he said quietly, which only emphasized his deliberate use of her full name all the more. "That's why I married you."

Blunt. And devastating. She nearly reeled from it.

This was what he'd been telling her since the beginning, but she'd been determined to connect the dots in a whole new way, creating a mess of an Impressionist painting that looked like *nothing* when she stepped back to view the whole. The spectacular kiss, the security system, the gentle concern—none of it had signaled anything special.

He'd meant what he said. He didn't *want* to invest energy in a relationship. That's why he cut himself off from people. Too much effort. Too much trouble. Too much fill-in-the-blank.

There was no friendship on the horizon, no tenderness, no progression toward intimacy. He expected her to get naked, get pleasured and get out. Eventually.

She nodded. "I see. We'll enjoy each other's company when we cross paths and then go our separate ways." *He'd* been the one euphemizing sex and she'd missed it.

Her heart twisted painfully. But this wasn't news. She just hadn't realized that being in a marriage that wasn't a marriage was worse than being alone.

How could Elise's computer have matched her with Leo? Oh, sure, neither of them had professed an interest in a love match, which was more of a tiny white lie in her case, but to not even be *friends?* It was depressing.

Leo looked relieved. "I'm glad we talked, then. To answer

your earlier question, you're everything I'd hoped. I'm very happy with my choice of wife. Jenna wasn't right at all."

Because she'd inadvisably bucked the rule: don't ask Leo for more than he chooses to give.

"Speaking of which," he continued, "I'd like you to plan a dinner party for twenty guests in about two weeks. Does that give you enough time?"

"Of course."

Two weeks?

Panic flipped her stomach inside out. How would she organize an entire party in two weeks? Well, she'd just have to.

This was why Elise matched her with Leo, and running his personal life was what she'd signed up for. She couldn't lose sight of that. "I'd be happy to handle that for you. Can you email me the guest list?"

He nodded. "Tommy Garrett is the guest of honor. Make sure you pick a date he's available. No point in having the party if he can't be there. Any questions?"

A million and five. "Not right now. I'll start on it immediately."

That was the key to enduring a marriage that wasn't a marriage. Jump into her job with both feet and keep so busy she didn't have time to castigate herself. After all, if she'd begun to believe this marriage might become more than an arrangement because of a few sparks, it was her fault. Not Leo's.

Her mother was being taken care of. Dannie was, too. Furthermore, she'd spoken her mind with as much blunt opinion as she could muster and Leo hadn't kicked her out. What else could she possibly want? This was real life, not a fairy tale, and she had work to do.

She bid Leo good-night, her head full of party plans. It wasn't until her cheek hit the pillow that she remembered the total discomfort on Leo's face when he thought friendship had been code for sex.

If he expected her to get naked, get pleasured and get out, why wouldn't he take immediate advantage of what he assumed she was offering?

Leo's forehead thunked onto his desk, right in the middle of the clause outlining the expiration date for his proposal to finance Miles Bennett's software company.

That woke him up in a hurry.

Why didn't he go upstairs to bed? It was 3:00 a.m. Normal people slept at this time of night, but not him. No—Leo Reynolds had superpowers, granting him the ability to go days without sleep, because otherwise he'd get behind. John Hu had slipped through his fingers at the alumni gala and was even now working with another backer. It should have been Leo. Could have been Leo, if he'd been on his game.

And not spending a good portion of his energy recalling his wife's soft and gorgeous smile. Or how much he enjoyed seeing her on the porch waiting for him, the way she had been tonight.

Sleep was for weaker men.

Younger men.

He banished that thought. Thirty-five—thirty-six in two months—wasn't old. But lately he felt every day of his age. Ten years ago he could have read contracts and proposals until dawn and then inhaled a couple of espressos to face the day with enthusiasm.

Now? Not so much. And it would only get worse as he approached forty. He had to make every day count while he could. No distractions. No seductive, tantalizing friendships that would certainly turn into more than he could allow.

Maybe he should up his workout regimen from forty-five minutes a day to an hour. Eat a little better instead of shoveling takeout into his mouth while he hunched over his desk at the office.

Gentle hands on his shoulders woke him.

"Leo," Daniella murmured as she pressed against his arm. "You fell asleep at your desk."

He bolted upright. Blearily, he glanced up at Daniella and then at his watch. Six-thirty. Normally he was already at work by now.

"Thanks for waking me up," he croaked and cleared his throat. "I don't know how that happened."

She lifted a brow. "Because you were tired?"

Her stylish dress was flowery and flirty, but clearly altered to fit perfectly, and her hair hung loose down her back. Flawlessly applied makeup accentuated her face and plumped her lips and he tore his gaze away from them.

"Besides that." He shuffled the Miles Bennett proposal back into some semblance of order without another glance at his wife. Though he wanted to soak in the sight of her. How did she look so amazing this early in the morning?

"Let me make you a cup of coffee," she offered and perched a hip on his desk as if she planned to stay awhile.

"I have to go. I'm late."

She stopped him with a warm hand on his bare forearm, below his rolled-up sleeve. "It's Saturday. Take ten minutes for coffee. I'd like to make it for you. Indulge me."

The plea in her eyes unhitched something inside. After he'd thrown up barrier upon barrier, she still wanted to make him coffee. How could he gracefully refuse? "Thanks. Let me take a quick a shower and I'll meet you in the kitchen."

The shower cleared the mist of sleep from his mind. He dressed in freshly pressed khakis and a button-down shirt instead of a suit since it was Saturday. A concession he couldn't recall making before. What had possessed him to do it today?

When he walked into the kitchen, the rich, roasted smell of coffee greeted him only a moment before his wife did.

She smiled and handed him a steaming mug. "Perfect timing."

He took a seat at the inlaid bistro table off the kitchen

and sipped. Liquid heaven slid down his throat. He wasn't surprised she'd somehow mastered brewing a cup of coffee to his tastes. "You even got the half-and-half right."

"Practice makes perfect." She slid into the opposite seat and folded her hands into her lap serenely.

Something in her tone piqued his interest. "How long have you been practicing?"

"Since the wedding." She shrugged, and her smile made light of the admission. "I've been trying to get up before you every morning so I could make you coffee. Today's the first day I succeeded."

The coffee didn't go down as smoothly on the next sip. Why had she put so much effort into something so meaningless? "That wasn't part of our agreement. You should sleep as late as you want."

"Our agreement includes making sure your life runs fluidly, especially at home. If you want coffee in the morning, it's my job to ensure you get it."

My job.

Daniella was in the employee box in his head, but he'd never expected her to view herself that way. Of course, why would she view herself any differently when all he talked about was their arrangement?

The cup of coffee—and the ironed clothes, ready at a moment's notice—took on implications of vast proportions. Everything EA International promised, he'd received. Daniella had slipped into her role as if she'd always been his wife. The staff liked her and already deferred to her judgment, which freed him from having to deal with the cook's grocery account or the gardener's questions about seasonal plants.

She was incredible.

If only he'd gotten the wife he really meant for EA International to match him with—one he could ignore—his life would be perfect.

It wasn't Daniella's fault he suffered from all-or-nothing syndrome. Intensity was the major backbone of his temperament. That's why he didn't draw anymore. Once he started, he could fill an entire notebook with landscapes, people's faces—Carmen's beautiful form—and then scout around for a blank book to begin filling that one, too.

If it hadn't been for his calculus teacher's timely intervention, Leo would probably be a starving artist right now, doodling in the margins of take-out menus and cursing the woman who'd been his first model. And his first lover. He'd been infatuated with capturing her shape on the paper, infatuated with her. His teacher had opened his eyes to his slipping grades, the upcoming SATs and a potentially bleak future mirroring his parents' if he didn't stop skipping school to draw Carmen. Fortunately, he'd listened and turned his intensity toward his education, then Reynolds Capital Management, vowing to never again let his obsessive personality loose on anything other than success.

He knew it the way he knew the sky was blue: the second he let himself taste Daniella again, that would be it. He wouldn't stop until he'd filled them both. And once wouldn't be enough. He'd be too weak to focus on anything except her.

"Thanks for the coffee. I should go." Leo shoved away from the table.

Her warm almond-colored eyes sought his. "Before you do, I have a couple of questions about the party for Tommy Garrett."

He settled back into the uncomfortable wrought-iron chair. "Sure."

It was the only subject that could have gotten him to stay. The party was critically important since Garrett had narrowed down the field to two firms. Leo didn't intend to lose out to the other guy.

She leaned forward on her forearms with all the attentiveness of someone about to leap into a negotiation. "What does Garrett Engineering make?"

Not *What china should I use?* or *What hors d'oeuvres should I serve?* "Why does that matter?"

"I'm curious. But also because I'd like to know more about the guest of honor. From you. I'll call his admin but I want your opinion. It will help me plan the menu and the decorations."

There was something hypnotic about Daniella's voice that pulled at him. He could listen to her recite the phone book. "I wouldn't have thought of that."

Her mouth tipped up in a smile that was so sweet, it pulled one from him. "That's why I'm here. Tell me."

"Tommy's a bit of a whiz kid." Leo pursed his lips as he contemplated the most relevant facets of the man—and he used the term *man* in the loosest sense—he wanted to do business with. "One of those geniuses who wears Converse sneakers and hoodies to work. He's just as likely to spout Xbox stats as engineering principles and no one cares because he graduated summa cum laude from Yale. He designed a modification to the way gasoline is consumed in a car that will increase gas mileage by almost double. It's revolutionary."

"You like him."

"Yes." The admission surprised him.

He hadn't thought one way or another about whether he *liked* Tommy Garrett. Leo liked the instant profitability of Garrett's design. He liked the idea of orchestrating the financing and letting Tommy be the face of the venture. Tommy had a lot of spirit, a quick wit and, despite the hoodies, he also had a work ethic Leo respected. It wasn't unusual to have a conversation at eleven o'clock on a Saturday night to brainstorm ideas.

Impressed, he cocked his head at his wife. "How did you ferret that out from what I said?"

"Because I listened with my eyes." Her smile widened as he snorted. "I could see it in your expression."

Leo tried to scowl but he was enjoying the back-and-forth just as much as the sound of Daniella's voice.

"It doesn't matter whether I like him. We stand to make a lot of money together and that's the key to our association. The party is paramount. He's got another potential partner on the hook and I need to convince him to go with Reynolds."

"What percentage stake in his company did you offer in the proposal?" He did a double take and she laughed. "I read up on how venture capital works. How can I help you land the deal if I don't know what I'm talking about?"

Perhaps he should have had a cup of coffee with his wife long before now. "I guess I thought you'd handle the party details and I'd handle Garrett. But I'm reconsidering that plan."

If he unleashed the formidable force of Daniella on Tommy Garrett, the poor guy probably wouldn't even know what hit him.

"You do that. Tell me more."

Her smile relaxed him. She had the best smile, easily given, genuine. He liked seeing it on her, but liked being the one to put it there even more. Making women smile wasn't a skill he felt particular proficient at, though. Maybe he should take a cue from his wife and practice.

"Not only will his design fit new engines, it retrofits to existing engines so it can be sold to both consumers and automobile manufacturers. It's almost miraculous. He might as well have designed a way to print money."

"Sounds like you really believe in the product. I can't imagine why Mr. Garrett would choose another venture capital firm."

"Because it's business. Not personal. And actually, I couldn't care less what the product is as long as the entrepreneur comes to me with a solid business plan and proven commitment."

"All business is personal, Leo," she said quietly. "If you

didn't spend so much time behind the scenes, you might discover that for yourself."

"Behind the scenes is where I function best." Ensuring the players never had to worry about money as they took center stage—that was his comfort zone. He couldn't afford to get truly involved or he'd bury himself.

Her expression softened, drawing him in. "But in the middle of things is where the best experiences are."

He had the distinct impression they weren't talking about Tommy Garrett anymore and had moved on to something he did not want to acknowledge in any way, shape or form.

"Thanks for the coffee. I'm going to head in to the office." He glanced at his watch. Almost seven-thirty, but there was no rush hour on Saturday, so he hadn't lost too much time. "If you have any more questions about the party, don't hesitate to call me."

"Have a good day." She covered his hand with hers and squeezed. "Don't look now, Leo, but I think we just had a friendly conversation. Are you shocked it didn't kill you?"

No, the shock happened when he laughed.

Her return smile stayed with him as he climbed into his car. The gas gauge needle pointed to full. When was the last time he'd even glanced at it? He drove to the office and instead of thinking about whatever else should be on his mind, he thought about Daniella.

Dannie. Maybe she could be Dannie and that wouldn't kill him, either.

No way. He couldn't imagine allowing it to roll from his tongue.

As much as he wished he could ignore his wife, he was painfully aware she conversely wished he wouldn't. They had an agreement, but it didn't seem to be sticking and she was flesh and blood, not a piece of paper. Or an employee.

And agreements could be terminated.

He was getting what he hoped from this marriage. She wasn't, not fully. If he wanted her to be happy, he had to give a little. Otherwise she might walk. A sick worm of insecurity wiggled into his stomach at the idea of losing a woman who fit into his life so well. And who, against all odds, he liked.

Friends. It didn't sound so terrible. Surely he could handle a friendship with his wife.

Six

Dannie hummed as she drew up proposed menus. She hummed as she perused the guest list Leo emailed her and savored the little thrill she got from the short message at the bottom.

You make a great cup of coffee.

She hummed as she waited on hold to speak with Tommy Garrett's admin and later as she checked off several more things on her to-do list. The tune was aimless. Happy. Half of it was due to finally connecting with Leo on some small level, especially after he'd made it clear he wasn't interested in developing their relationship.

The other half had to do with finding her niche. Growing up, her chief source of entertainment had been old movies and TV shows on the free channels, and she'd always wanted to have her own household like the glamorous women of the '50s. It was everything she'd expected. Being in charge of her domain gave her a heady sense of accomplishment and purpose, which popped out of her mouth in song.

When Leo strode through the door at six o'clock that evening with a small, lopsided grin, her throat seized up and quit working entirely.

"I thought we'd have dinner together," he said as she stared at him, wordless. "If you don't have other plans."

Dinner? *Together?* Why?

"Oh," she squeaked and sucked in a couple of lungfuls

of oxygen in hopes it might jar everything else into functioning. "No plans. I'll let the cook know."

Clothes, she thought as she flew to alert the staff Leo would be dining in. She should change clothes. And open a bottle of wine. Her foot tangled on the edge of the Persian runner lining the stairs to the second floor. *And slow down.* A broken leg wouldn't do her any favors.

This was the first time she'd dine alone with Leo since they'd gotten married. It was practically like a date. Better than a date, because it had been his idea and totally a surprise. She wanted it to be flawless and so enjoyable he couldn't wait to do it again.

In spite of a triple-digit pulse and feeling as though her tongue was too big for her mouth, she could get used to that kind of surprise.

Dannie opened her closet and surveyed her small but lovely wardrobe. She'd never owned such amazing clothes and shoes before and never got tired of dressing up. She slipped into a casual black cocktail dress that veed over her breasts, buckled her feet into the sexiest Louboutins she owned and curled her lip at the state of her hair. Quickly she brushed it out and twisted it up into a sleek chignon.

Done. That was as close as she could get to looking like the kind of wife a man would enjoy coming home to. She took her time descending the stairs in her five-inch heels and spent a few minutes in the wine cellar glancing at labels until she put her hand on a sauvignon blanc *Wine Spectator* had talked up. A perfect date-night wine.

She stuck the bottle in a bucket of ice and left it on the formal dining room sideboard to chill until dinner, which the cook informed her would be a few minutes yet. At loose ends, she tormented the place settings until the silverware was either perfectly placed or exactly where it'd been when she started. She couldn't tell, which meant *stop obsessing.*

The cook announced dinner at last. She went to fetch Leo and found him in his study, of course, attention decisively on his laptop. His suit jacket hung on the back of the leather chair. His shirtsleeves were rolled up on his forearms and he'd already removed his tie. Rumpled Leo might be her favorite.

Leaning on the doorjamb, she watched him type in efficient strokes, pause and type again. Mentoring anonymously via chat again, most likely. She hated to interrupt. But not really.

"Dinner's ready."

He glanced up without lifting his head and the way he peeked out from under his lashes was so sexy, it sent a spiral of heat through her tummy.

"Right now?" he asked.

"Um, yeah." She cleared the multitude of frogs camping out on her vocal cords. "We don't want it to get cold."

He typed for another couple of seconds and then closed the laptop's lid with a snick as he stood. "That would be a shame."

Boldly, she watched him approach, aware her body blocked the doorway and curious what he'd do about it. "I'm a believer in hot food, myself."

He stopped a healthy distance away when he apparently realized she wasn't budging. "I'm looking forward to a home-cooked meal. Thought I should start eating better. I've had too much takeout lately."

Whose fault is that? "Just the food, then? The company wasn't a draw?"

"Of course the company was a factor." Something flickered in the depths of his blue eyes and heat climbed all over her.

Oh, that had all sorts of interesting possibilities locked inside. They gazed at each other for a long, delicious moment, and he didn't look away. Or back up.

Then he gestured to the hall. "Shall we, Mrs. Reynolds?"

And somehow, that was far more intimate than calling her Dannie. Deliberate? Oh, goodness, she hoped so.

Leo's capable palm settled into the small of her back as they walked and she felt the contact all the way to the soles of her feet. Something had changed. Hadn't it? Was her coffee *that* good?

In the dining room, Leo drew back the heavy chair and allowed her to sit on the brocade cushion before pushing it in for her. Then he expertly poured the wine to exactly the same level in both glasses on the first try—impressive evidence of how good Leo was with both detail and his hands.

Not that she'd needed additional clues the man hid amazing things under his workaholic shell. Were they at a point where she could admit how outrageously attracted to Leo she was? Or was that going past blunt into another realm entirely?

Placing her glass on the table before her, he took the seat catercorner to hers instead of across the table. "So we can talk without shouting," he said when she raised her eyebrows.

All small, small gestures, but so huge to her romance-starved soul. Flutters spread from her stomach to every organ in her body. Especially her heart.

For whatever reason, he was trying, really *trying,* to give her some of his time. But what was his intent? The friendship she'd hoped for or merely a small gesture toward crossing her path?

She'd keep her wits about her and under no circumstances would she read anything into what was essentially just dinner. As they dug into Greek salads served with crusty bread, she stuck to discussing her progress on the party. The more the wine flowed, the more relaxed they both became.

About halfway through her swordfish, she brought up the one thing she'd been dying to ask since the night of their marriage. "Do you still draw?"

Leo's fork froze over a piece of grilled zucchini. "How did you know about that?"

"Your mother told me."

He grimaced. "I should have guessed. She still has every piece of paper I've ever touched with a pencil."

Which was no answer at all. "Is it a sensitive subject?"

"No." Carefully, he cut a hunk of fish and chewed it in a spectacular stall tactic she recognized a mile away. He didn't want to discuss his art, that much was clear.

"So, never mind then. It's not important," she lied. His reaction said there was more to the story and it was very important, but she didn't want to alienate him. "Tell me something else instead. Why venture capital?"

His expression warmed. "If you're good, you can make a lot of money. You just have to recognize the right opportunities."

"Are you good?"

She already knew the answer but was curious what he thought about the empire he'd built. Most of her research into the complexities of venture capital had been conducted by reading articles about her husband's successful company before she'd even spoken to him on the phone for the first time.

"I'm competent. But I've made my share of mistakes."

As if that was something to be ashamed of. He seemed determined to downplay all his positives. "Everyone makes mistakes. You've recovered from yours quite well. The reputation of Reynolds Capital Management is unparalleled."

He inclined his head with a pleased smile. "It's a work in progress."

Fascinated with the way his eyes turned deeper blue when he engaged, she drained her wineglass and propped her chin on a curled hand. This was exactly what she'd envisioned their friendship would look like. "So how do you recognize the right opportunity?"

The cook bustled in and cleared their empty dinner plates, replacing them with bananas Foster for dessert. She lit the rum and blew it out in an impressive culinary display, then efficiently disappeared.

Leo spooned the dessert into his mouth and murmured appreciatively before answering Dannie's question. "Experience. Gut instinct. A large percentage of success is simply showing up. I create the remaining percentage by getting there first and staying until everyone else has gone home."

"Do you see your job as creative?" Dannie took a small bite of banana, gratified Leo liked the dessert as much as she did, but determined to keep him engaged in conversation. A full mouth wouldn't lend itself well to that.

He pursed his lips. "In a way, I suppose. Without backing, a lot of entrepreneurs' ideas would never see the light of day. I provide the platform for other people to tap into their creativity."

Which was what he'd done for her—given her the opportunity and the means to be exactly what she wanted to be. A wife. If tonight was any indication, Leo had changed his mind about spending time getting to know each other. Maybe she'd get the relationship—in some form or fashion—she craved out of it, too.

"You're the puppet master, then," she said.

"Not at all. I never stick my fingers in the pie. Micromanagement is not the most effective way to do business. I'm the money, not the talent."

"But you have talent," she protested.

His expression dimmed. "You've never seen one of my drawings."

"I meant you have a talent for recognizing the right opportunity." She smiled in hopes of keeping things friendly. "But I have a feeling you've got artistic talent, too. Draw me something and I'll let you know."

She was pushing him, she knew she was. But she wanted to know him, and his mysterious artistic side intrigued her.

"I don't draw anymore," he said, the syllables so clipped they nearly drew blood.

Message received. They hadn't connected nearly as deeply as she'd hoped, but they'd only just begun. One day, maybe he'd open up that part to her. "You've moved on to bigger and better canvases. Now you're creating your art with completely different tools."

Leo pushed his chair back. "Maybe. I've got some work to finish up. Thanks for dinner."

He escaped, leaving her to contemplate whether to open another bottle of wine in celebration of a successful dinner or to drown her disappointment since Leo had abandoned her once again.

Drown her disappointment. Definitely.

She located a bottle of pinot that went better with her mood than white wine and filled her glass almost to the rim. Then she called her mother to talk to someone uncomplicated and who she knew loved her always and forever, no matter what.

"Dannie," her mother cried when she answered. "Louise just told me. Thank you!"

Dannie grinned. Her mother's caregiver had turned into a friend almost instantly, and the two were constantly chattering. "Thanks for what?"

"The cruise, silly. The Bahamas! I'm so excited, I can hardly stand it." Her mother clucked. "I can't believe you kept this a secret, you bad girl."

The wineglass was somehow already half-empty again, but she didn't think she'd drunk enough to be *that* confused. "I didn't know. What cruise?"

"Oh. You don't? Louise said Leo booked us on a seven-day cruise, leaving out of Galveston. Next week. I thought for sure you suggested it. Well, thank him for us. For me, especially."

A steamroller flattened her heart. Her husband was a startling, deeply nuanced man underneath it all.

Dannie listened to her mother gush for several more minutes and managed to get a couple of sentences in sideways in spite of the question marks shooting from her brain. Were Leo's nice gestures indicative of deeper feelings he didn't want to admit for some reason? No man did a complete about-face without a motive. Had he come home for dinner in hopes of developing a friendship—or more?

Regardless, *something* had changed, all right, and her husband owed her a straight answer about what.

Sometimes talking to Leo was worse than pulling teeth, like their conversation after her text about the fake noise. Her marriage didn't just call for blunt—if she wanted to get answers, it apparently called for Scarlett, as well. And Scarlett had been squashed up inside for a really long time.

Three glasses of wine put a good dose of liquid courage in Dannie's blood. She ended the call and cornered Mr. Behind the Scenes in his office.

She barged into the study. Leo glanced up, clearly startled. She rounded the desk to pierce him with the evil eye, not the slightest bit concerned about the scattered paperwork under his fingers.

"About this cruise." Bumping a hip against the back of his chair, she swiveled it so he faced her, swinging his knees to either side of hers.

Not the slightest bit intimidated, he locked gazes with her. "What about it?"

Good gravy, when he was this close to her, the man practically dripped some sort of special brand of masculinity that tightened her thighs and put a tingle between them.

"Are you going to deny you did something nice for my mother?"

"No?" He lifted his brows. "Or yes, depending on whether *you* thought it was nice, I suppose."

His voice hitched so slightly, she almost didn't notice it until she registered the rising heat in his expression. *Oh, my.* That was lovely. Her proximity was putting a tingle in his parts, too.

"It was nice. She's very excited. Thank you."

He sat back in his chair, as if trying to distance himself

from the sizzling electricity. "Why do you seem a little, ah, agitated?"

"Agitated." She inched forward, not about to give up any ground, and her knees grazed the insides of his thighs. "I *am* agitated. Because I don't get why you won't ever acknowledge the wonderful things you do."

His gaze flicked down the length of her body and back up again slowly. "What would be the point of that?"

Her husband was nuanced all right...and also incredibly frustrating. He likely refused to take credit for his actions because that would require too much of an *investment* from him. Someone might want to reciprocate and make him feel good, too, and then there'd be a whole cycle of emotions. *That* would never do.

She huffed out a noise of disgust and poked him in the chest, leaning into it as her temper rose. "You do these things and it's almost like you'd prefer I didn't find out you've got a kind streak. Jig's up, Leo."

He removed her finger from his rib cage, curling it between his and holding it away from his body instead of releasing it. Probably so she wouldn't wound him, but his skin sparked against hers and nearly buckled her knees.

The memory of *that kiss* exploded in her mind and heightened the gathering heat at her core.

But she still didn't know what was happening between them—friends, lovers, more? Maybe it was actually none of the above. If she gave in to the passion licking through her, would he disappear afterward until the next time he wanted sex? Or could this be the start of something special?

"You have an active imagination," he said.

She rolled her eyes to hide the yearning he'd surely see in them. "Yeah, I get it. You're a ruthless, cold-blooded businessman who'd rather be caught dead than disclosing your real name to a couple of students. What's it going to take to get you off the sidelines and into the middle of your own life?"

That was the key to unlocking his no-emotional-investment stance on marriage. It had to be. If he'd only wade into the thick of things and stop cutting himself off, he'd see how wonderful a real relationship could be. How satisfying. Fulfilling. Surely their marriage could be more than an occasional crossing of paths. He needed her to help him see that.

Leo's frame tensed and slowly he rose from the chair, pushing into her space. "I like the sidelines."

Toe-to-toe, they eyed each other, the impasse almost as palpable in the atmosphere as the swirl of awareness. "Why did you book my mother on a cruise?"

He shrugged, lashes low, shuttering his thoughts from her. "I thought she would like it."

"That's only half the truth. You did it for me." A huge leap. But she didn't think she was wrong.

Their gazes locked and the intensity shafted through her. "What if I did?"

Her pulse stuttered. Coffee, then dinner. Now this. What was he trying to accomplish? "Well, I'm shocked you'd admit that. Before you know it, we'll be buying each other birthday cards and taking vacations together. Like real couples."

Like the marriage of her dreams. Just because neither of them had expressed an interest in a love match didn't mean it was completely impossible to have found one. What better security was there between two people than that of knowing someone would love you forever?

He threw up a palm. "Let's don't get out of hand now."

She advanced, pushing his palm into her cleavage, burning her skin with his touch and backing him against the desk. She wanted to bond with her husband in the most elemental way possible. To complete the journey from A to B and see what they really could have together.

"I like getting out of hand."

"Do you have a response for everything?" His fingertips curled, nipping into her skin.

"If you don't like what I have to say, then shut me up."

His expression turned carnal. He watched her as he slid an index finger down the valley between her breasts and hooked the neckline of her dress. In a flash, he hauled her forward, capturing her lips in a searing kiss.

On legs turned to jelly, she melted into it, into him as he wrapped his arms around her, finally giving her what she'd been after since she walked in. Maybe since before that.

Greedy for all of him, she settled for the small, hot taste of Leo against her mouth. With a moan, she tilted her head and parted his lips with hers. She plunged into the heat, seeking his tongue with hers, and he obliged her with strong, heated licks.

His arms tightened, crushing her against his torso, aligning their hips. Need soaked her senses as his hard ridge nudged her. She cupped the back of his neck as his hand snaked under her dress to caress the back of her thigh.

Yes. As seduction techniques went, he could teach a class.

Soft cotton skimmed under her fingers as she explored the angles and muscles of his back. Delicious. Her husband's body was hard and strong, exactly as she liked, exactly perfect to keep her safe and satisfied at the same time.

The kiss deepened and the hand on her thigh inched higher, trailing sparkling warmth along with it. She tilted her hips in silent invitation, begging him to take those fingers wherever he so desired.

But then he pulled away, chest heaving, and spun her to face the wall, his torso hot against her spine.

"Daniella," he murmured in her ear, and his fingertip traced the line of her dress where it met the flesh of her back, toying with the zipper. "I'm about to pull this down and taste every inch of you until we're both mindless. Is that what you want?"

Damp heat flooded her and she shuddered. "Only if you call me Dannie while you do it."

He strangled over a groan and moved her forward a confusing foot, then two. "I can't do this."

"Don't say you don't want me." *So close. Don't back off now.* She whirled and tilted her chin at the bulge in his pants she'd felt branding her bottom. "I already know that's not true. You don't kiss someone like that unless you mean it."

"That's the problem." Breath rattled in his throat on a raw exhale. "You want me to mean it in a very different way than I do mean it. I'd rather not disappoint you and that's where this is headed. Making love will not change the fact that tomorrow I'm still going to work a sixteen-hour day, leaving little time for you. Until both of us can live with that, I need you to *walk away.*"

He was blocking himself off from her again, but for a very good reason. The rejection didn't even bother her. How could it? He was telling her he didn't want to treat her like a one-night stand.

That set off a whole different sort of flutter.

"I'm walking." *For now.* She needed a cooler head—among other parts—to navigate this unexpected twist to their marriage.

She skirted the desk, putting much-needed distance between them.

Raking a hand through his hair, he sank into the chair with a pained grimace. "Good night."

"This was the best date I've ever been on."

With that parting shot, she left him to his paperwork, already plotting how to crack that shell open a little wider and find the strong, amazing heart she knew beat beneath. He thought they were holding off until she was okay with no-emotional-investment sex, but he was already so emotionally invested, he was afraid of hurting her.

That's what had changed. Somehow, she had to help him see what he truly needed from her.

If a large percentage of success happened by showing up and then outwaiting the competition, she could do that. Yes, her competition was an intangible, unfathomable challenge called *work,* but the reward compensated for the effort.

Time for a little relocation project.

Seven

The silky feel of Daniella's thigh haunted Leo for days. And if he managed to block it from his mind, her fiery responses when he kissed her replaced that memory immediately.

It didn't seem to matter how many spreadsheets he opened on his laptop. Or how many proposals for new ventures he heard. Or whether he slept at the office because he lacked the strength to be in the same house with Daniella. Sleeping as a whole didn't work so well when his wife invaded his unconscious state to star in erotic dreams.

There was no neat, predefined box for her. For any of this. It was messing him up.

He hadn't seen Daniella in four days and the scent of strawberries still lingered in his nose.

Fingers snapped before his eyes and Leo blinked. Mrs. Gordon was at his desk, peering at him over her reading glasses. "I called your name four times."

"Sorry. Long night."

Mrs. Gordon's gaze flicked to the other end of Leo's office, where a sitting area overlooked downtown Dallas. "Because that couch is too short for a big, strapping young man like you."

He grinned in spite of being caught daydreaming, a mortifying situation if it had been anyone other than his admin. "Are you flirting with me?"

"Depends. How much trouble are you in at home?" Her

raised eyebrows wiped the smile off his face. "Enough that an old woman looks pretty good right about now?"

"I'm not in trouble at home. What does that even mean? You think I got kicked out?" He frowned.

It bothered him because deep down, he knew he'd taken the coward's way out. Being friends with his wife hadn't worked out so well. She was too sexy, too insightful.

"Au contraire. You're in trouble. It's all over your face."

"That's ridiculous." Leo scrubbed his jaw, not that he believed for a second he could erase whatever she thought she saw there, and fingered a spot he'd missed shaving that morning. The executive bathroom off his office left nothing to be desired, but two hours of sleep had affected his razor hand, apparently.

"Forget her birthday, did you?" Mrs. Gordon nodded sagely.

Soon we'll be buying each other birthday cards, Daniella had said, but he didn't even know when her birthday was. "Our marriage isn't like that."

Mrs. Gordon's mouth flattened. Her favorite way to remind him she had his number. "Why do I get the feeling you and your wife have differing opinions about that?"

He sighed and the hollow feeling in his stomach grew worse because she was right. "Did you hear from Tommy Garrett's people yet?"

"Don't change the subject. I'd have told you if I heard from Garrett and you know it. Just like you know you've got a problem at home that you better address sooner rather than later. I've been married for thirty years. I know things." She clucked. "Take my advice. Buy her flowers and sleep in your own bed tonight."

He had the distinct impression Mrs. Gordon believed his wife would be in the bed, as well. He didn't correct her.

After all, what sort of weakness did *that* reveal?

He couldn't have sex with his own wife because he'd backed himself into an impossible corner. She wanted some kind of intimacy, which he couldn't give her, and he didn't want to hurt her. He'd thought friendship might be enough, but friends apparently talked about aspects of themselves that he just couldn't share. Especially not drawing. It was tied to his obsessive side, which he kept under wraps.

How long would Dannie remain patient before finding someone who *would* give her what she wanted? Women in his life usually lasted about two months before bailing.

He'd never cared before. Never dreamed he'd experience moments of pure panic at the thought of Daniella going the way of previous companions. They had a convenient marriage, but that meant it would be easy to dissolve when it was no longer convenient for her.

By 9:00 p.m., Leo couldn't argue with his admin's logic any longer. His body screamed to collapse in a dead sleep, but he couldn't physically make himself lie down on that couch.

What was he really accomplishing by avoiding his wife? When he'd told her to walk after nearly stripping her bare right there in his study, she had. No questions, no hysterics, no accusations. She was fine with holding off on advancing their relationship.

Daniella wasn't the problem. He was.

He was a weak daydreamer who'd rather scratch a pencil over pieces of paper all day and then spend several hours exploring his wife's naked body that night. And do it again the next day, abandoning all his goals with Reynolds Capital Management in a heartbeat for incredible sex and a few pictures. He'd done exactly that before, and he feared the consequences would be far worse if he did it with Daniella.

If he could resist the lure of drawing, he could resist the Helen of Troy he'd married. As long as he didn't kiss her again, he had a good shot at controlling himself. Of course, the real problem was that deep down, he was pretty sure he didn't want to.

He drove to the house he'd bought with his own money,

where he'd created a safe, secure home that no one could take away. The lights always shone brightly and the boiler always heated water. And Leo would die before allowing that to change.

Daniella wasn't downstairs. Good. Hopefully she was already asleep in her room. If so, he could get all the way to his bedroom without running into her.

As he passed the study, his neck heated as the dream from last night roared into his mind—the one where he finished that kiss from the other night by spinning Daniella facedown onto the desk, pushing up that sexy dress and plunging into her wet heat again and again until she convulsed around him with a cry.

That room was off-limits from now on. He'd buy a new desk and have it moved into his bedroom.

So exhausted he could hardly breathe, he climbed the stairs and stumbled to his bedroom. No lights. Too bright for his weary eyes.

His shin cracked against something heavy and knocked him off balance. He cursed as his hand shot out to break his fall and scraped across…whatever he'd tripped over.

Snick. Light flooded the dark room via the lamp on his bedside table.

"Are you okay?" Daniella asked.

His head snapped up in shock. "What are you doing here? Why are you in my bed?"

His wife, hair swept back in a ponytail and heavy lidded with sleep, regarded him calmly from beneath the covers of *his bed.* "It's my bed, too, now. I moved into your room. If you'd come home occasionally, you might have known I rearranged the furniture."

The throb in his shin rivaled the sudden throb in his temples. "I didn't… You ca—" He sucked in a fortifying breath. "You had no right to do that."

She studied him for a moment, her face contemplative and breathtakingly beautiful in its devoid-of-makeup state.

"You said I should think of this as my home. Anything I wanted to change, you'd be willing to discuss."

"Exactly. *Discuss.*"

The firm cross of her arms said she'd gladly have done so, if he hadn't been hiding out at the office.

"You're bleeding." She threw the covers back, slipped out of bed and crossed the room to take his hand, murmuring over the shallow cut.

As she was wearing a pair of plaid pants cinched low on her slim hips and a skintight tank top that left her midriff bare, a little blood was the least of his problems.

"And you're cold," he muttered and tore his gaze from the hard peaks beneath the tank top, which scarcely contained dark, delicious-looking nipples.

Too late. Heat shuddered through his groin, tightening his pants uncomfortably. Couldn't she find some clothes that she wasn't in danger of bursting out of? Like a suit of armor, perhaps?

"I'll be fine." She tugged on his hand, flipping the long ponytail over her shoulder. "Come into the bathroom. Let me put a bandage on this cut."

"It's not that bad. Go back to bed. I'll sleep somewhere else." As if he had a prayer of sleep tonight.

Adrenaline coursed through his veins. Muscles strained to reach for her, to yank on the bow under her navel and let those plaid pants pool around her ankles. One tiny step and he could have her in his arms.

He tried to pull away but she clamped down on his hand, surprisingly strong for someone so sensuously built.

"Leo." Her breasts rose on a long sigh and under her breath she muttered something about him that sounded suspiciously uncomplimentary. "Please let me help you. It's my fault you're hurt."

It was her fault he had a hard-on the size of Dallas. But it was not her fault that he'd been avoiding her and thus didn't know the layout of his own bedroom any longer. "Fine."

He followed her into the bathroom, noting the addition of a multitude of mysterious girly accoutrements, and decided he preferred remaining ignorant of their purposes.

Daniella fussed over him, washing his cut and patting it dry. In bare feet, she was shorter than he was used to. Normally she had no trouble looking him in the eye when she wore her architecturally impossible and undeniably sexy heels. He hadn't realized how much he liked that.

Or how much he'd also like this slighter, attentive Daniella who took care of him. Fatigue washed over him, muddling his thoughts, and he forgot for a second why it wasn't a good idea to share a bed with her.

"All better." She patted his hand and bent to put the box of bandages under the sink, pulling her pajama pants tight across her rear, four inches from his blistering erection. He closed his eyes.

"About the room sharing," he began.

She brushed his sensitive flesh and his lids flew up. He'd swayed toward her, inadvertently. She glanced up to meet his gaze in the mirror. The incongruity between her state of undress and his buttoned-up suit shouldn't have been so erotic. But it was.

"Are you going to read me the riot act?" she asked, her eyes enormous and guileless and soft. "Or consider the possibilities?"

"Which are?" The second it was out of his mouth, he wished he could take it back. Foggy brain and half-dressed wife did not make for good conversation elements.

"You work a hundred hours a week. Our paths will never cross unless we do it here." She gestured toward the bedroom. "This way, we'll both get what we want."

In the bright bathroom light, the semitransparent tank top left nothing to the imagination. Of course, he already knew what her bare breast looked like and the longer she stood there with the dark circles of her nipples straining against the fabric, the more he wanted to see them both, but this time with no interruptions.

"What do you think I want?"

"You want me." She turned to face him. "All the benefits without the effort, or so you say. I don't believe you. If you wanted that, my dress wouldn't have stayed zipped for longer than five seconds after dinner. Sharing a bedroom offers you a chance to figure out why you let me walk away. It won't infringe on your work hours and it gives me a chance to forge the friendship I want. Before we become physically involved."

That cleared the fog in a hurry. "What are you saying, that you'll be like a *roommate?*"

"You sound disappointed." Her eyebrows rose in challenge. "Would you like to make me a better offer?"

Oh, dear God. She should be negotiating his contracts, not his lawyer.

"You're driving me bananas. No. Worse than that." He squeezed the top of his head but his brain still felt as though she'd twirled it with a spaghetti fork. "What's worse than bananas?"

"Pomegranates," she said decisively. "They're harder to eat and don't taste as good."

He bit back a laugh. Yes, exactly. His incredibly perceptive wife drove him pomegranates. "That about covers it."

"Will you try it my way? Give it a week. Then if you still think sex will complicate our marriage too much, I'll move back to my bedroom. I promise I'll keep my hands to myself." To demonstrate, she laced her fingers over her sexy rear and he swore. She'd done that exact thing in one of his dreams. "If you'll promise the same."

His shin didn't hurt nearly as badly as his aching groin. "Are you seriously suggesting we share a bed platonically?"

"Seriously. Show me you think our marriage is worth it. Sharing a room is the only way we'll figure this out, unless you plan to work less. It's unorthodox, but being married to a workaholic has forced my creative hand, so to speak."

It was definitely creative, he'd give her that, and hit him where it hurt—right where all the guilt lived. If he wanted her to be happy in this marriage and stick with him, he had to prove it.

Her logic left him no good reason not to say yes. Except for the fact that it was insane.

Her seductive brown eyes sucked him in. "What are you going to do, Leo?"

Somehow, she made it sound as if he held all the cards. As if all he had to do was whisper a few romantic phrases in her ear and she'd be putty in his hands. If only it was that easy.

And then she shoved the knife in a little further. "Try it. What's the worst that can happen?"

He groaned as several sleepless nights in a row hit him like a freight train. "I'm certain we're about to find out."

Fatigue and a strong desire to avoid his wife's backup plan if he said no—that was his excuse for stripping down to a T-shirt and boxer shorts and getting into bed next to a woman who blinded him with lust by simply breathing. Whom he'd agreed not to touch.

Just to make her happy. Just for a few days. Just to prove he wasn't weak.

He fell into instant sleep.

Dannie woke in the morning quite pleased but quite uncomfortable from a night of clinging to the edge of the bed so she didn't accidentally roll over into Leo's half. Or into Leo.

She'd probably tortured him enough.

But her will wasn't as strong as she thought, not when her husband lay mere feet away, within touching distance, breathing deeply in sleep. The alarm on his phone had beeped, like, an hour ago, but hadn't produced so much as a twitch out of Leo. Who was she to wake him when he obviously needed to sleep? A good wife ensured her husband was well rested.

The view factored pretty high in the decision, too.

Goodness. He was so gorgeous, dark lashes frozen above his cheekbones, hair tousled against the pillow.

How in the world had she convinced him to sleep in the same bed with her *and* agree to hold off on intimacy? She'd thought for sure they'd have a knock-down-drag-out and then he'd toss her out—bound and determined to ignore his own needs, needs he likely didn't even recognize. But instead of cutting himself off from her again, he'd waded right into the middle of things like she'd asked, bless him.

Because his actions spoke louder than words, and his wife was an ace at interpreting what lay beneath.

If this bedroom sharing worked out the way she hoped, they'd actually talk. Laugh over a sitcom. Wake up together. Then maybe he'd figure out he was lying to himself about what he really wanted from this marriage and realize just how deeply involved he already was.

They'd have intimacy—physically and mentally. She couldn't wait.

She eased from the bed and took a long shower, where she fantasized about all the delicious things Leo would do when he finally seduced her. It was coming. She could feel it.

And no matter how much she wanted it, anticipated it, she sensed she could never fully prepare for how earthshaking their ultimate union would truly be.

When she emerged from the bathroom, Leo was sitting up, rubbing the back of his neck, and her mouth went dry. Even in a T-shirt, he radiated masculinity.

"Good morning," she called cheerfully.

"What happened to my alarm?" He did not look pleased.

"I turned it off after listening to it chirp for ten minutes."

"Why didn't you wake me up?"

"I tried," she lied and fluttered her lashes. "Next time would you like me to be a little more inventive?"

"No." He scowled, clearly interpreting her question to mean she'd do it in the dirtiest, sexiest way she could envision.

"I meant with a glass of water in your face. What did you think I meant?"

He rolled his eyes. "So this is what roommates do?"

"Yes. Until you want to be something else."

With that, she flounced out the door to check off the last few items on the list for Tommy Garrett's party. It was tomorrow night and it was going to be spectacular if she had to sacrifice her Louboutins to the gods of party planning to ensure it.

Leo came downstairs a short while later, actually said goodbye and went to work.

When he strolled into the bedroom that evening, the hooded, watchful gaze he shot her said he'd bided his time all day, primed for the showdown about to play out.

"Busy?" he asked nonchalantly.

Dannie carefully placed the e-reader in her hand on the bedside table and crossed her arms over her tank top. What was it about that look on his face that made her feel as if she'd put on Elise's red-hot wedding night set? "Not at all. By the way, I picked up your dry cl—"

"Good." He threw his messenger bag onto the Victorian settee in the corner and raked piercing blue eyes over her, all the way to her toes tucked beneath a layer of Egyptian cotton. They heated, despite the flimsy barrier, and the flush spread upward at an alarming rate to spark at her core.

What had she been talking about?

He shed his gray pin-striped suit jacket and then his tie. "You caught me at a disadvantage last night. I had a few other things on my mind, so I missed a couple of really important points about this new sleeping arrangement."

Her relocation project had just blown up in her face. He was good and worked up over it.

"Oh? Which ones?" The last syllable squeaked out more like a dolphin mating call than English as he dropped his pants, then slowly unbuttoned his crisp white shirt. What had she done to earn her very own male stripper? Because she'd gladly do it fourteen more times in a row.

"For starters, what happens if I don't keep my hands to myself?"

The shirt hit the floor and her jaw almost followed. Her husband had quite the physique hidden under his workaholic shell.

So maybe he wasn't mad. But what was he?

Clad in only a pair of briefs, Leo yanked the covers back and slid into his side of the bed. She peeled her gaze from his well-defined chest and refixed it on his face, which was drawn up in a slight smirk, as if he'd guessed the direction of her thoughts. Her cheeks flamed.

"I'll scold you?" She swallowed as he casually lounged on his pillow, head propped on his hand as if settling in for a nice, long chat instead of using those hands to do something far more…intimate. "I mean, it wouldn't be very sporting of you."

"Noted." He stretched a little and the covers slipped down his torso. "What happens if *you* don't keep your hands to yourself?"

He was toying with her, seeing if he could get her to break her own vow of chastity. In his thoroughly male mind, he'd be in the clear if *she* made the move. His eyelids dropped to a very sexy half-mast and sizzled her to the core.

"And Daniella? Be sure you spell really well so it's all very clear for those of us who didn't barge into someone else's bed and start slinging rules around."

Actually, the relocation project might be working better than she'd assumed. At least they were talking. Now to get him to understand this wasn't a contest. Their relationship was at a crossroads and he had to choose which fork he wanted to take.

"There are no rules," she corrected. "I don't have a list of punishments drawn up if you decide you're not on board with being roommates, whether you want to go back to separate bedrooms or strip me naked right now. You're calling the shots. You're the one who shut it down after dinner the other night. *Walk away,* you said, and I did, but that's not what either of us wanted."

"Yeah?" Lazily, he traced the outline of her shoulder against the propped-up pillow at her back, carefully not touching her skin but skating so close the heat from his finger raised every hair on her body. "What would you rather I have told you to do?"

"No games, Leo." She met his gaze squarely. "I'm giving us an opportunity to develop a friendship. But I also readily admit I want you. I want your mouth on me. Here." Just as lazily, she traced a line over her breast and circled the nipple, arching a little. "I want it so badly, I can hardly stand it."

She watched him, and went liquid as his expression darkened sinfully.

"No games?" he asked and cleared the rasp from his throat. "Then what is this?"

"A spelling lesson." And she obviously had to really lay it out for him. She dropped her hand. "You want me, then come and get me. Be as emotionally naked as you are physically. Strip yourself as bare as your body and let's see how fantastic it can be between us."

Stiffening, he closed off, his expression shuttering and his body angling away. "That's all? You don't ask for much."

"Then forget I mentioned it. We don't have to hold out for a connection that may not ever happen. If either of us becomes uninterested in the hands-to-yourself proposition I laid out, it's off." She flung herself back against the pillow, arms splayed wide. "Take me now. I won't complain. We'll have sex, it'll be great and then we'll go to sleep."

He didn't move.

"What's the matter?" she taunted, glancing at him sideways. "It's just sex. Surely you've had just sex before. No brain required. I have no doubt a man with your obvious, um…*talent* can make me come in no time at all. In fact, I'm looking forward to it. I'm hot for you, Leo. Don't make me wait a second longer."

"That's not funny. Stop being ridiculous." Translation: he didn't like being thoroughly trounced at his own game.

She widened her eyes. "Did you think I was joking? I'm not. We're married. We're consenting adults. Both of us have demonstrated a healthy interest in getting the other naked. We'll eventually go all the way. It's your choice what sort of experience that will be."

This had never been about withholding sex. She'd be naked in a heartbeat as soon as he made a move. All the power was in his hands and when that move came, it would be monumental. And he'd be so very, very aware of exactly what it meant.

He shoved both hands through his hair. "Why is it my choice?"

Poor, poor man. If he was too clueless to know she didn't have a choice, far be it from her to fill him in. This was something he had to figure out on his own. Besides, he was the one with the crisis of conscience that prevented him from making love to her until something he probably couldn't even articulate happened.

But she knew exactly what he needed—to let himself go. She'd exploit this situation gladly in order to get the marriage she desperately wanted and help him find the affection and affinity he so clearly yearned for.

She smiled. "Because. I'm—" *Already emotionally invested.* "—generous that way."

She was going to drag Leo off the sidelines kicking and screaming if that's what it took to have the love match she sensed in her soul Elise had actually orchestrated.

Eight

By nine o'clock, the party hummed along in full swing, a success by anyone's account. Except perhaps Leo's. In the past hour, he'd said no more than two words to Dannie.

She tried not to let it bother her as she flitted from group to group, ensuring everyone had a full glass of champagne and plenty to talk about. The final guest list had topped out at twenty-five and no one sent their regrets. Chinese box kites hung from the ceiling, artfully strung by the crew she'd hired. Their interesting geometric shapes and whimsical tails provided a splash of color in the otherwise severe living room. A papier-mâché dragon lounged on the buffet table, breathing fire under the fondue pot in carefully timed intervals.

Tommy's admin had mentioned his love of the Orient and the decorations sprang easily from that. More than one guest had commented how unusual and eye-catching the theme was, but Tommy's signature on the dotted line was the only praise she needed.

Well, she'd have taken a "You look nice" from Leo. The ankle-length black sequined dress had taken three shopping trips to find and a white-knuckle twenty-four hours to alter. She'd only gotten it back this morning and it looked great on her.

Not that anyone else had noticed.

She threw her shoulders back and smiled at the knot of

guests surrounding her, determined to be the hostess Leo expected.

Hyperawareness burned her back on more than one occasion, and she always turned to see Leo's piercing blue eyes on her and his expression laced with something dangerous.

The bedroom-sharing plan was a disaster. He hated it. That had to be his problem—not that she'd know for sure, because he'd clammed up. Was he waiting until the party was over to give her her walking papers?

Turning her back on Leo and the cryptic bug up his butt, she came face-to-face with Leo's friend Dax Wakefield. "Enjoying the party?" she asked him brightly.

Not one person in this room was going to guess she had a mess of uncertainty swirling in her stomach.

"Yes, thank you." Unfailingly polite, Dax nodded, but his tone carried a hint of frost. "The buffet is wonderful."

Her radar blipped as she took note of the distinct lack of a female on Dax's arm. A good-looking guy like Dax—if you liked your men slick and polished—was obviously alone by choice. Was he no longer dating Jenna? Or had Leo asked him not to bring her in some misguided protective notion?

"I'm so glad." She curved her lips graciously and got nothing in response. Maybe he was aloof with everyone. "Congratulations again on the distinguished alumni award. Leo assures me it was well deserved."

"Thank you." Not one hair on his perfectly coiffed head moved when he granted her a small nod. "Took me a little longer to achieve than Leo. But our industries are so different."

What did that mean? There was an undercurrent here she couldn't put her finger on, but Dax definitely wasn't warming up to her. *Problem alert.* Dax and Leo were old friends and a wife was a second-class citizen next to that. Was Dax the genesis of Leo's silent treatment?

"Well, your media empire is impressive nonetheless. We watch your news channel regularly." It wasn't a total lie—

Leo had scrutinized stock prices as they scrolled across the bottom of the screen last night as she pretended to sleep after the spelling lesson.

Dax smiled and a chill rocked her shoulders. If Leo wanted people to believe he was a ruthless, cold-blooded businessman, he should take lessons from his friend. That guy exuded *take no prisoners*.

One of the servers discreetly signaled to get her attention and she pounced on the opportunity to escape. "Will you excuse me? Duty calls."

"Of course." Dax immediately turned to one of Leo's new partners, Miles Bennett, and launched into an impassioned speech about the Cowboys roster and whether they could make it to the Super Bowl this time around.

The server detailed a problem in the kitchen with several broken champagne bottles, which Dannie solved by pulling out Leo's reserve stash of Meunier & Cie. It was a rosé, but very good and would have to do in a pinch. Most of the guests were men and such a girly drink had definite potential to go over like a lead balloon.

Mental note—next time, buy extra champagne in case of nervous, butterfingered staff.

She poured two glasses of the pink champagne and sought out Tommy Garrett. Something told her he'd take to both an out-of-the-norm drink and being roped into a coconspiracy.

Maybe because of the purple canvas high-tops he'd worn with his tuxedo.

"Tommy." Grateful she'd caught him alone by the stairs, she handed him a champagne flute. When Leo had introduced them earlier, they'd chatted for a while and she'd immediately seen why her husband liked him. "You look thirsty. Humor me and drink this. Pretend it's beer."

A brewery in the Czech Republic exported Tommy's vice of choice, which she'd gleaned from his admin. But he'd already had two pints and hopefully wouldn't balk at her plea.

The young man flipped chin-length hair, bleached almost white by the sun, out of his face. "You read my mind. Talking to all these suits has parched me fiercely."

Half the champagne disappeared into Tommy's mouth in one round and he didn't gag. A glance around the room showed her that others weren't tossing the rosé into the potted plants. Crisis averted.

"Thanks, Mrs. Reynolds." She shot him a withering glare and he winked. "I mean Dannie. Sorry, I forgot. Beautiful women get me all tongue-tied."

She laughed. "Does that geek approach actually work?"

"More often than I would have ever imagined. Yet I find myself devoid of promising action this evening." Tommy sighed dramatically and waggled his brows, leaning in to murmur in her ear. "Wanna see my set of protractors sometime?"

Her grin widened. She really liked him, too, and was almost disappointed he hadn't worn a hoodie to her fancy party. "Why, Thomas Garrett, you should be ashamed of yourself. Hitting on a married lady."

"I should be, but I'm totally not. Anyway, I couldn't pry you away from Leo with a crowbar and my own private island. Could I?" he asked hopefully with a practiced once-over she suspected the coeds fell for hook, line and sinker.

"Not a chance," she assured him. "I like my men all grown-up. But feel free to keep trying your moves on me. Eventually you'll become passable at flirting with a woman."

Tommy clutched his heart in mock pain. "Harsh. I think there might be blood."

That prickly, hot flash traveled down her back an instant before Leo materialized at her elbow. His palm settled with familiarity into the groove at her waist and she clamped down on the shiver before it tipped him off that such a simple touch could be so affecting. *Why* had she worn a backless dress?

"Hey, Leo." Tommy lifted his nearly empty glass in a toast. "Great party. Dannie was telling me how much she likes protractors."

"Was she, now?" Leo said easily, his voice mellower than the scotch in his highball.

Uh-oh. She'd never heard him speak like that.

Swiping at Tommy with a flustered hand, she glanced up at Leo and nearly flinched at the lethal glint in her husband's eyes. Directed at her or Tommy? "Protractors. Yes. They get the job done, don't they? Just like Leo. Think of him as a protractor and Reynolds's competitor, Moreno Partners, as a ruler. Why not use the right tool for the job from the very beginning?"

Tommy eyed her. "Moreno is pretty straight and narrow in their approach. Maybe that's what I need."

Good, he'd picked up on her desperate subject change.

"Oh, no." Dannie shook her head and prayed Leo's stiff carriage wasn't because he didn't like the way she was sticking her nose in his business with Tommy. This was absolutely what she was here for and she absolutely didn't want to blow it, especially with Leo in such a strange, unpredictable mood. "Reynolds can help you. Leo's been doing this far longer than Moreno. He has connections. Expertise. You know Leo has a degree in engineering, too, right?"

Leo's hand drifted a little lower. His pinky dipped inside her dress and grazed the top edge of her panties. Her brain liquefied into the soles of her sparkly Manolos and she forgot to mention he'd actually double majored in engineering and business.

"Daniella," Leo murmured. "Perhaps you'd see to Mrs. Ross? She's wandering around by the double glass doors and I'm afraid she might end up in the pool."

"Of course." She smiled at Tommy, then at Leo and went on the trumped-up errand Leo had devised, likely to avoid saying outright in front of a prospective partner that he could handle his own public relations. Which she appreciated.

As she guided Mrs. Ross toward the buffet, she laughed at the sweet old lady's jokes, but kept an eye on Leo and Tommy. They were still talking near the stairs and Leo's expression had finally lost that edge she so desperately wanted to understand.

If she'd gone too far with the bedroom-sharing idea, why didn't he just tell her?

This party was a measure of how effectively she could do her job as Leo's wife and how well she contributed to his success. Coupled with the high-level tension constantly pulsing between them, her nerves had stretched about as tight as they could without snapping.

Dannie showed the last guest to the door and spent a long thirty minutes with the auxiliary staff wrapping up postparty details.

Leo was nowhere to be seen.

Around midnight, she finally stumbled to their bedroom with the last bottle of champagne, uncorked, intending to split it with him in celebration of a successful party. Surely Leo shared that opinion. If he didn't, she really should be told why.

Darkness shrouded the bedroom.

She set the champagne bottle and two glasses on the dresser and crossed to the freestanding Tiffany torchiere lamp in the corner. She snapped it on and bracing against the wall, fingered apart the buckle on one shoe.

"Oh, you should leave those on." Leo tsked, his voice silky as scotch again.

She whirled. He was lounging on the settee, tie loose and shirt unbuttoned three down. Not that she was counting. "What are you doing sitting here in the dark?"

"Seemed appropriate for my mood."

That sounded like a warning. She thumbed off the other shoe in case she had to make a run for the door. "Would you like me to turn off the light?"

He contemplated her for a long moment. "Would darkness make it easier for you to pretend I was Tommy Garrett?"

She couldn't help it. The laugh bubbled out.

It was a straight-from-the-bottle kind of night. Retrieving the champagne from the dresser, she gulped a healthy dose before wiping her mouth with the back of one hand. "Jealousy? That's so…" *Cliché.* Well, it seemed like a tell-it-like-it-is night, too. "…cliché, Leo."

His gaze scraped her from head to toe, darkening as he lingered at the vee of her cleavage. "What should I feel while watching my wife flirt with another man?"

"Gratitude?" she offered. "I was working him for you."

Leo barked out a laugh. "Shall I call him back, then? See if he's up for a threesome?"

This was going downhill fast. Not only was he not thrilled with her party, he'd transformed into a possessive husband. "Are you drunk?"

Maybe she should catch up. If she downed the entire bottle of champagne, her husband might make a lot more sense. Or it would dull the coming rejection—which this time would no doubt include an annulment. Alcohol had the potential to make either one more bearable.

"Not nearly drunk enough," he muttered. Louder, he said, "Since you're so free with your favors this evening, perhaps you'd do me another one."

Her eyes narrowed. "Like what?"

"Show me what's under that dress."

Okay, *not* the direction she'd anticipated him going. *More champagne, STAT.* She swigged another heady gulp and set the bottle on the dresser. "Why? So you can stake your claim? Jealousy is not a good enough reason to strip for you."

His mouth quirked. "What would be?"

"Diamonds. A trip to Bora-Bora. A Jaguar." She ticked

them off on her fingers airily. If he was going to be cliché, she could, too. "The typical kept woman baubles."

"What if I called you…Dannie?" He drew it out and in that silky voice, it swept down her spine and coalesced in her core with heat. "It's the key to intimacy, isn't it? You let Tommy call you that. The two of you were very cozy."

She cursed under her breath. How dare he turn her on while accusing her of dallying with Tommy? "He's twenty-four, Leo. I'm old enough to be his…older sister. Stop being such a Neanderthal."

"So that's your objection to Tommy? His age?" Leo slid off the settee and advanced on her, slowly enough to trip her pulse. "What about Dax? He's my age. Maybe you'd like him better."

"What's this really about?" Boldly, she stared him down as he approached, determined to get past this barrier she sensed he'd thrown up to avoid the real issue—she'd failed at being the wife he needed, on all levels. Somehow. "You're not threatened by Tommy. Or Dax. You've been weird all evening. If you've got a problem with me, lay it out. No more smoke and mirrors."

Only a breath away, he halted, towering over her. Without heels, she wasn't that much shorter than he was, but his presence—and his dark, intense mood—overwhelmed her.

"You know, I do have a problem with you." His gaze traveled over her and that's when she saw the vulnerability he'd hidden behind a mask of false allegations. "You're still dressed."

Baffled, she cocked her head and studied him. Hints of what he was so carefully not telling her filtered through. All at once, she realized. He *was* threatened by other men and conversely paralyzed by his conscience, which had dictated that he wouldn't touch her until she was okay with what he could give.

His body language was equally conflicted. His fingers

curled and uncurled repeatedly, as if he wanted to reach for her but couldn't.

She was his wife. But not his wife, in the truest sense.

Her heart softened. He wanted something he had no experience with, no vocabulary to define. And she'd been trying to force him into admitting his needs by sharing his bed and denying him the only outlet for his emotions that he understood, assuming her way was best.

Well, this was all new to her, too, but she wasn't above changing course to give him what he needed.

Their connection was already there. Instead of waiting on some murky criteria she doubted either of them could verbalize, she'd just show him.

That was a good enough reason to strip for him.

Dannie locked her gaze on his and reached up to her nape to unclasp her dress.

Leo was acting like an ass.

Knowing it didn't give him any better ability to control it, or to eliminate the constant spike of lust when he caught sight of his wife. Seeing her laugh with another man had generated something ugly and primal inside.

He didn't like it.

He didn't like how he'd focused so much energy and attention on this deal with Tommy Garrett and then spent the night sulking in the corner instead of using the opportunity to do his job. His wife had picked up the slack. *His wife.* Once again, she'd kept the importance of the evening front and center while he wallowed in jealousy.

How dare she be so perfect and imperfect at the same time?

A few more fingers of scotch might have dulled the scent of strawberries. But he doubted it. When he was this close to his wife, nothing could dilute the crushing awareness.

Daniella's fingers danced across the back of her neck. His gut clenched as he realized what she was doing, but the protest died in his throat as her glittery dress waterfalled off her body, catching at the tips of her breasts for one breathless second. Then it puddled on the floor, baring her to his greedy gaze.

A beautiful, half-nude vision stood before him. Daniella, in all her glory. Fire raged south, ravaging everything in its path to his center, numbing his extremities and nearly bringing him to his knees.

It would be fitting to kneel before a goddess.

"Daniella." His raw voice scraped at his throat and he cleared it. "What are you doing?"

He knew. She was doing what he'd been pushing her to do. But she was supposed to slap him. Or storm out. Or push him in kind, the way she always did. As long as she punished him for being an ass, any response would have been fine.

Except this. And it was a far more suitable penance to get exactly what he asked for.

"I'm eliminating the problems," she said, head held high. "*All* the problems."

That was impossible, let alone this way. "Put your clothes back on. I'm—"

Actually, he had no clue what he was. Nothing could have prepared him to feel so…ill equipped to be in the same room with a woman who radiated power and sensual energy.

He shut his eyes.

Strip yourself as bare as your body, she'd suggested. But his wife's simple act of disrobing, of making herself vulnerable, had accomplished that for him, even while he was still fully dressed.

Everything about her touched him in places no one had ever dared tread.

This night was not going to end well. She wanted something he couldn't allow himself to give her. Once that bottle was uncorked, he'd focus on nothing but Daniella and lose his drive to succeed. Then he'd fail her—and himself—on a whole different level, which he could not accept.

"Leo." The softness in her voice nearly shattered him. "Open your eyes. Look at me."

He did. God help him, but he couldn't resist. His gaze sought hers, not the gorgeous bare breasts there for his viewing pleasure. His eyes burned with effort to keep them trained straight ahead.

"I would never—" she emphasized the word with a slash of her hand "—dishonor you with anyone else, let alone a friend or a business partner. I respect you too much. I'm sorry if I behaved in a way that made you question that."

Her words, sweetly issued and completely sincere, wrenched that hollow place inside. He'd been treating her horribly all night for who knew what reason and she was apologizing. "You didn't. You were just being a good hostess."

A very poor depiction of how absolutely stellar a party she'd thrown. She deserved far more than degradation at the hands of her husband. Far more than the absent, unavailable man she'd cleaved to.

"I really hope you think so." Her expression warmed. "You're the only man I want. Forever. That's why I married you."

The sentiment flowed like warm honey through his chest. This was the kind of romantic nonsense he'd gone to EA International to avoid. But then, wasn't she describing exactly what he'd asked for? Fidelity and commitment? It just sounded like so much *more* than that from her mouth, so deep and profound.

What was he supposed to do with that? With her?

"Don't you want me, too?" she asked, her voice dropping into a seductive whisper that funneled straight to his erection.

"So much more than I should," he muttered and regretted saying it out loud.

"Then come over here and show me."

His feet were rooted to the carpet. It wasn't going to be just sex. Maybe just sex wasn't possible with someone he'd made his wife.

Regardless, he'd married Daniella, and consummating their relationship meant they were embarking on forever at this very moment.

Part of him strained to dash for the door, to down the rest of the scotch until the unquenchable thirst for Daniella faded from memory. Then he wouldn't have to deal with the other part that compelled him to accept everything she was offering him, even the alarming nebulous nonphysical things.

"So the touching moratorium is lifted?" he asked. "Or is this the precursor to another round of rules?"

Apparently he wasn't finished lashing out at her. If he infuriated her enough to leave, they could go back to circling each other and he'd put off finding out exactly how weak he was.

He didn't want her to leave.

"This is about nothing more than being together. Do whatever feels right to you." She spread her arms, jutting out her perfectly mounded breasts. His mouth tingled and he imagined he could taste one. "Standing here in nothing other than a tiny thong is turning me into Jell-O. I'd really like it if you'd kiss me now."

"A thong?" He'd been so focused on her front, the back hadn't even registered. The feel of silk beneath his pinky when he'd pushed past the fabric at her waist during the party rushed back and he groaned.

Slowly, she half turned and cocked a hip, bare cheek thrust out. "I wore it for you. Hoping you'd pick tonight to make me your wife in more than name only."

He was so hard he couldn't breathe. Let alone walk. Or kiss. Neither was he ready to cross that line, to find out how far she'd suck him down the rabbit hole if he gave in to the maelstrom of need.

Her lips curved up in a secret, naughty smile. Palms flat against her waist, she smoothed them downward over the curve of her rear, down her thighs. "If you're not going to touch me, I'll just do it myself."

Provocatively, she teased one of her nipples with an index finger. Her eyes fluttered halfway closed in apparent pleasure and he swore. Enough was enough.

She was serious. No more choices, rules, games or guidelines. She wanted him.

It was too late to address all the lingering questions about the status of their relationship or how this would change it. It was too late to imagine he'd escape, and far too late to pretend he wanted to.

Daniella was going in the lover box. Now.

In one stride, he crossed the space between them and swept her up in his arms. He swallowed her gasp a moment before his lips captured hers. Crushing her against him, he leaped into the carnal desire she'd incited all night. Actually, since that first glimpse of her on the stairs at their wedding. Every moment in between.

Their mouths aligned, opened, fed. Eagerly, she slid her tongue along his, inviting him deeper. He delved willingly, exploring leisurely because this time there'd be no interruptions.

He was going to make Daniella his, once and for all. Then he'd recover his singular concentration and no more deals would slip away as he daydreamed.

The taste of her sang through his veins and instead of weakening him, she gave him strength. Enough strength to pleasure this woman until she cried out with it. Enough to grant her what she'd been begging for. Enough to make love to her all night long.

He'd hold on to that strength, because he'd need it to walk away again in the morning. It was the only outcome he'd allow, to delve into the physical realm without losing himself in it. Just tonight, just once.

Leo broke the kiss long enough to pick her up in his arms. Carefully, he laid her out on the bed and spent a long moment drinking in the panorama of his wife's gorgeous body. All that divine skin pleaded for his touch, so he indulged himself, running fingertips down her arms, over the peaks and valleys of her torso and all the way down to her siren-red toenails.

He glanced at her face. She was so sensuously lost in pleasure, his pulse nearly doubled instantly.

She shivered.

"Cold?" he asked.

Shaking her head, she got up on her knees and pulled his tie free. "Hot. For you."

Then she slid off his jacket and went to work on the buttons of his shirt, watching him as she slipped them free.

Finally, she'd completely undressed him. Taking her in his arms, he rolled with her to the middle of the bed and picked up the kiss where they'd left off.

Her lips molded to his and his mind drained as her warm body snugged up against him. They were naked together, finally. Physically, at least.

Almost naked. He skimmed a hand down her spine and fingered the thong. Silky. Sexy. She'd worn it for him. If he'd known that, the party would have been over at about seven-thirty.

Her palm raced across his skin in kind and her touch ignited an urgency he couldn't allow. He'd take as little pleasure from this as possible. Otherwise he'd never leave the bed. It was a delicate balance, made more complicated by the fact that no matter what she'd said, she still wished for something cataclysmic out of this.

He'd make it as physically cataclysmic as he could. That was the best he could do.

Still deep in her mouth, he yanked off the thong and then explored her torso with tiny openmouthed kisses until he reached her core. There, he licked her with the very tip of his tongue.

"Leo," she gasped, which only drove his urgency higher.

"You taste like heaven." He wanted more and took her nub in his mouth to nibble it gently, then harder, laving his tongue against it until she writhed beneath his onslaught.

Mewls deep in her throat attested to her mindless pleasure and then she cried, "More. I'm about to come," which was so hot it shoved him to the brink.

His erection pulsed and he clamped down, aching with the effort to keep from exploding. He drove a finger into her wet core, then two, and tongued her and she arched up as she clinched around him, shattering into a beautiful climax.

He rose up and tilted her chin to soak up the sated, satisfied glint in her eyes as he gave her a minute to recover. But not too long. When her breathing slowed a bit, he guided her hands upward and curled them around the top edge of the headboard.

If she touched him, he'd lose all his hard-won control.

"Hold on," he murmured, and she did, so trusting, so eager.

He parted her thighs and slowly pushed into her. Rapture stole across her face, thrilling him. She enveloped him like a vise, squeezing tight. She was amazing, open, wet.

His vision flickered as Daniella swamped his senses.

More. He thrust into her. *Again.*

Desire built, heavy and thick, and he thumbed her nub, circling it. Heat broke over him and he ached to come but needed her to come first. To prove he wasn't weak, and that he could still resist her.

"Daniella," he ground out hoarsely, and she captured his gaze.

He couldn't break free.

Everything shrank down to this one suspended moment and her bottomless, tender irises ensnared him, encouraging him to just feel. And he did feel it, against his will, but heaviness spread alarmingly fast through his chest, displacing what should be there. Against all odds, she'd wrenched something foreign and indefinable and magnificent from his very depths.

Only one thing could encapsulate it, one word. "Dannie."

It left his mouth on a broken plea and she answered with a cry, convulsing around him, triggering his release. He poured all his desire, all his confusion—and what he feared might be part of his soul—into her, groaning with sensual gratification he'd never meant to experience.

Daniella had taken his name, taken his body. Taken something primal and physical and turned it into poetry. The awe of it engulfed him, washing through his chest. He wanted to mark every page of her again and again and never stop. And let her do the same to him.

Intellectually, he'd realized long ago that one small taste of her would never be enough. But the actual experience had burst from its neat little box, crushing the sides, eclipsing even his wildest fantasies.

He couldn't allow himself to indulge like that again. Otherwise his wife would swallow him whole and take every bit of his ambition with her.

Nine

Dannie awoke at dawn tangled with Leo. Her husband, in every sense.

Muscles ached and begged to be stretched so beautifully again. Above all, her heart longed to hear him say "Dannie" with such raw yearning as they joined. Like he had last night, in that smoking-hot voice.

The bedroom-sharing plan deserved an award.

Leo was still asleep, but holding her tightly against him with his strong forearms, her back against his firm front. The position seemed incongruous for someone so determined to remain distanced. But in sleep, his body told her what he couldn't say with his mouth.

He craved a relationship with her, too. The yearning bled from him in waves every moment she spent in his company. It was all over the good deeds he did behind the scenes, which she no longer believed were designed to avoid emotional investment.

He just didn't know how to reach out. And she'd gladly taken on the job of teaching him.

As he guided her toward her full potential as his wife, she'd done the same, pushing him to keep opening up, giving him what he needed. She'd keep on doing it until he embraced everything this marriage could be. The rewards of being the woman behind the man were priceless.

She hated to disturb him, but his front was growing

firmer by the moment and it pressed hot and hard against her suddenly sensitized flesh.

Heat gathered at the center of her universe and her breath caught.

Involuntarily, her back arched, pushing her sex against his erection. She rubbed back and forth experimentally. Hunger shafted through her. Oh, *yes*.

Then his whole body stiffened and his hands curled against her hips, forcing her to be still. Awake, and obviously not on board with a round of morning love.

Wiggling backward, she deliberately teased him without words.

"Daniella," he murmured thickly. "Stop. I forgot to set my alarm. I have to go to work."

"Yes, you do." She wiggled again, harder, and he sucked in a ragged breath. "Ten minutes. I'm so turned on, I'm almost there already."

Cool air rushed against her back as he rolled away and left the bed without another word.

Her heart crashed against her ribs as he disappeared into the bathroom. The shower hummed through the walls.

Nothing had changed between them.

Last night had meant everything to her. But she'd vastly overplayed her hand. Instead of viewing it as a precious stepping-stone toward a fulfilling marriage, Leo seemed perfectly content to sleep with her at night and ignore her the rest of the day.

Exactly what he'd warned her would happen.

She had no call to be disappointed. She'd given him what he needed and hoped it would be the beginning of their grand, sweeping love affair. It obviously wasn't. She'd dropped her dress, pushed him into making that final move and, for her effort, got a round of admittedly earth-shattering sex. She'd even given him permission to do whatever felt right.

At what point had she asked for anything more?

Since the *I do*s, she'd put considerable effort into preventing screwups, convinced each successful event or household task solidified her role as Mrs. Reynolds.

It never occurred to her the real screwup would happen when she invented a fictional future where Leo became the husband of her dreams.

Flinging the covers up over her shoulder, she buried herself in the bed, dry-eyed, until Leo left the bedroom without saying goodbye.

Then she let her eyes burn for an eternity, refusing to let the tears fall.

Her stupid phone's musical ringtone split the air. *Leo.*

Bolting upright, she bobbled the phone into her hands. He was calling to apologize. Tell her good morning. That it had been a great party. Something.

A bitter taste rose at the back of her throat when she saw *Mom* on the caller ID. She swallowed and answered.

"Hi," she said and her voice broke in half.

"What's wrong, baby?"

Great, now her mother was concerned. Worrying her mother was the last thing Dannie wanted.

"Nothing," she lied brightly. "I'm still in bed. Haven't woken up yet. How are you?"

"Fine." A round of coughing negated that. "Do you want to have lunch today?"

Oh, that would never do. Her mother would instantly see the hurt in her heart blossoming on Dannie's face. She had to get over the disenchantment first. "I've got a few things to do. Maybe tomorrow?"

"I'm leaving on the cruise tomorrow. Did you forget? I wanted to see you before I go."

Yes, she had forgotten and it was a brutal reminder about what was important—her mother. Not Dannie's bruised feelings.

Suck it up, honey. "I can rearrange my appointments. I'll pick you up around eleven, okay?"

"Yes! I'll see you then."

Dannie hung up, heaved a deep shuddery breath and hit the shower to wash away every trace of Leo from her body. If only she could wipe him from her mind as easily, but his invisible presence stained the atmosphere of the entire house.

She fought tears for twenty excruciating minutes as the car sped toward her mother's.

The driver paused at the curb outside her mother's apartment and Dannie frowned. Paint peeled from the wood siding and weeds choked the grass surrounding the front walk. The shabbiness had never bothered her before. How was it fair that Dannie got to live in the lap of luxury but her mother suffered both pulmonary fibrosis and near poverty?

But what could Dannie do about it? She didn't have any money of her own—everything was Leo's. A nasty voice inside suggested he could pony up alternative living space for her mother in reciprocation for last night.

She hushed up that thought immediately. Leo hadn't treated her like that. He'd told her what would happen on more than one occasion and she'd chosen to create a fairy tale in her head where love conquered all.

Her mom slid into the car and beamed at Dannie. The nurse had done wonders to improve her mother's quality of life with daily pulmonary therapy and equally important emotional support.

"I'm so glad to see you, baby," her mom gushed.

The driver raised the glass panel between the front seat and the back, then pulled out into the flow of traffic to ferry them to the restaurant. Dannie leaned into her mother's cheek buss and smiled. "Glad to see you, too."

What ills could she possibly have that Mom couldn't make all better? The pricking at her eyelids grew worse.

Her mother's hands on her jaw firmed. "Uh, oh. What happened?"

She should have known better—sonar had nothing on a

mom's ability to see beneath the surface. Dannie pulled her face from her mother's grasp and looked out the window in the opposite direction. "Nothing. Leo and I had a little… misunderstanding. I'll get over it."

Probing silence settled on her chest and she risked a glance at her mother. She was watching her with an unreadable expression. "Nothing serious, I hope."

Dannie half laughed. "Not in his opinion."

With a sigh of relief, her mother settled back against the seat. "That's good."

"Well, I don't think he's planning to divorce me, if that's what you're worried about."

At least not yet. By all rights, her desperate mental reorganization of their arrangement should have resulted in a firm boot to the backside long before now. Yet, he hadn't breathed a word about divorce, so apparently he still needed her for reasons of his own.

"Of course that's a concern." Her mother's warm hand found Dannie's elbow. "Fortunately, you married a solid, respectable man who believes in commitment. A very wise choice. You'll never end up brokenhearted and alone like I did."

Yes. That was the purpose of this marriage. Not grand, sweeping passion and a timeless love. This was a job. Wife was her career. Hardening her heart against the tiny tendrils of feelings she'd allowed to bloom last night in Leo's arms, Dannie nodded. "You're right. Leo is a good man."

The muted sound of sirens filtered through the car's interior a moment before an ambulance whizzed by in the opposite direction. She'd ridden in an ambulance for the first time not too long ago, on the way to the hospital, with her mother strapped to a gurney and fighting to breathe. When the bill came, she'd gone to the library that same day seeking a way to pay it.

And now she was riding in the modern-day equivalent

of a horse-drawn carriage, but better because it had air-conditioning and leather seats.

Leo had saved them both, providing security for her and for her mother. She couldn't lose sight of that again. He'd held up his end of the bargain honestly. It was time for her to do the same and stop wallowing in the mire of lost romance that she'd never been promised in the first place.

Love didn't work out for other people. Why would it be any different for her?

"The misunderstanding wasn't over the possibility of children, was it?" her mother asked.

Hesitantly, Dannie shook her head.

They hadn't used protection. Actually, she could be pregnant right now. Warmth soaked through her chilled soul. If Leo gave her a child, his absence would be notably less difficult. Her mother had raised her single-handedly. Dannie could do that, too.

Funny how she hadn't thought about procreation once last night. Yet children had been foremost on her mind when she'd agreed to marry Leo. Back when she assumed there was no possibility of more between them than an arrangement. Now she knew for a fact there was no possibility.

Suck it up. She pasted on a smile for her mother. "Tell me more about the cruise."

Her mother chatted all through lunch and Dannie responded, but couldn't have repeated the content of their discussion for a million dollars. Fortunately, Leo didn't come up again. That she would have remembered.

Leo didn't call and didn't join her for dinner. She got ready for bed, resigned to sleeping alone.

At ten o'clock, he strolled into the bedroom.

Her gaze flicked over him hungrily, searching for small clues to the state of mind of the man who'd put his lips on her body in very inventive ways not twenty-four hours ago.

"Hi," she said politely and flicked off the TV she'd been

staring at for who knew how long with no idea what was on. "How was your day?"

"Fine," he said. "I got you something."

Her eyebrows rose. "Like a present?"

Lifting the small silver gift bag clutched in his fingers, he nodded and crossed to the bed to hand it to her. She spilled out the contents and opened the square box. Diamond earrings sparkled against royal-blue velvet.

The box burned her hand and she threw it on the bedside table. "Thank Mrs. Gordon for me. She has lovely taste."

His face instantly turned into a brick wall. "I spent an hour picking them out myself. To thank you for the party. You were amazing. I should have told you before now."

"I'm sorry." Remorse clogged her throat. What had happened to the quiet, demure girl Elise created? Lately, Dannie rarely thought twice about what came out of her mouth. "That was obnoxious."

"And well earned." He cleared his throat and sought her gaze, his blue eyes liquid. "I'm sorry I left the way I did this morning. That was *far* more obnoxious. And undeserved."

"Oh." He'd robbed her of speech. Which was probably fortunate, since the question on the tip of her tongue was, *Why* did *you leave that way, then?* She didn't ask. If he'd intended for her to know, he'd have told her.

Regardless, he'd apologized. *Apologized.* And bought her a present.

Leo retrieved the box and handed it to her. "Will you wear the earrings? I'll take them back if you don't like them."

A touch of the vulnerability she'd witnessed last night darted across his expression. The earrings represented both a thank-you and an apology and he wanted her to like them. Just when she thought she had the dynamic between them straight in her head, he flipped it upside down.

"I love them." She unscrewed the backs and stuck them in her ears, then struck a pose. "How do they look?"

"Beautiful." His gaze skittered down her body and back up again. He wasn't even looking at her ears.

A wealth of undisclosed desire crackled below the surface. Some of it was physical. But not all. He'd picked out the earrings himself. What did that mean? She'd lay odds *he* didn't even know what the significance of that was.

Last night, she'd learned one surefire way to communicate with him.

She flung back the covers and crawled to him. He watched her, his body poised to flee, but she snagged his lapels before he could. Without speaking, she peeled his jacket from his shoulders and teased his lips with hers as she unknotted his tie.

"Daniella." He groaned against her lips and pulled back a fraction. "The earrings weren't… I'm not—"

"Shh. It's okay." The tie came apart in her hands and she leaned into him, rubbing his chest in small circles with her pebbled nipples.

Almost imperceptibly, he shook his head. "I don't expect sex in exchange for jewelry."

How could such a simple statement sink hooks so deeply into her heart? He was trying so hard to be honorable, so hard to keep from hurting her at great expense to himself. "And I don't expect jewelry in exchange for sex. Now that's out of the way. Shut up and put your hands on me."

His eyelids flew closed and he swallowed. That was close enough to a yes for her. She bridged the gap and claimed his lips with hers.

Winding the ends of his tie around her hands, she pulled him closer and deepened the kiss. A firestorm swept outward from their joined lips, incinerating her control.

Urgently, wordlessly, she undressed him, desperate to bare Leo in the only way he'd allow. He ripped off her pajamas and they fell to the bed already intertwined.

Leo kissed her and it was long and thorough. *This* was the man who'd held her in his sleep. The man who'd whispered her name with gut-wrenching openness. As she'd known beyond a shadow of a doubt, this joining of bodies spoke volumes beyond the scope of mere words. And it said Leo had far more going on beneath the surface than he dared let on.

As she cradled her husband's beautiful body and stared into the depths of his hot-with-passion blue eyes, something blossomed inside. Something huge and reckless, and she tamped it down with no small effort. But it rose up again, laced with images of Leo's child growing in her womb. She imagined the tenderness of his gaze as he looked down on their newborn child and the back of her throat heated.

Suddenly, the fear of Leo tiring of her romantic foolishness wasn't her only problem anymore.

She'd traded it for the painful, diametrically opposite problem of what was going to happen if she fell in love with him and doomed herself to a lifetime of marriage to a man who would forever keep his kind heart buried beneath a workaholic shell.

Tap. Tap. Tap.

Leo blinked and glanced up. Dax tapped his pen a few more times, his face expressionless as he nodded to the laptop screen filled with verbiage regarding the proposed joint venture to finance a start-up company called Mastermind Media.

"Clause two?" Dax prompted and lowered a brow. "They agreed to extend the deadline to midnight. We don't have long. You were supposed to be telling me why you don't like it."

I don't like it because it's standing between me and a bed with my wife in it.

Theoretically, that applied to the entire proposal he and Dax had been tearing apart since four-thirty with only a short break for General Tso's chicken in bad sauce from Jade Dragon.

Leo stole a peek at his watch. Nine o'clock on a Friday night.

If he left the office now, he could be home in twenty minutes. Sixteen if he ignored the speed limit. He might even text Daniella as he drove to let her know he'd be there soon. Maybe she'd greet him wearing nothing but the diamonds he'd given her.

What started as a simple thank-you gift had somehow transformed into something else. Hell if he knew what. He hadn't intended to make love to her again. At least not this soon, not while he was still struggling to maintain some semblance of control around her.

But one minute Daniella was threading the diamonds through her ears, and the next...

The memory of last night and his sexy wife invaded his mind. Again. The way she'd been doing all day.

"The clause is fine." *No.* It wasn't. Leo shook his head and tried to focus. "It will be fine. With a minor tweak to the marketing expectations."

More tapping. Then Dax tossed down his pen with a sense of finality.

"Leo." Dax shrank down in the high-backed chair and laced his hands over one knee, contemplating the ebony conference table. Lines appeared across his forehead. "I'm starting to get the impression you don't think we should do this deal."

"What?" Leo flinched. *No more daydreaming.* What was wrong with him? "I've put in sixty hours on this. It's a solid proposal."

"Then what's up?" His friend eyed him, concern evident in his expression. "We've been looking at Mastermind Media for months. If you're worried about you and me doing business together, you should have spoken up long before now."

Hesitating, Leo rolled his neck. They'd known each other

more than fifteen years—since college. Dax was the one person who'd call him on it if Leo zoned out. "That's not it."

"Is the financing sticky?" Dax frowned, wrinkling his pretty-boy face. "You're not using your own money on this because of our relationship, are you?"

"Of course not." Venture capital relied on other people's money. Leo never risked anything he didn't have to.

"I've run out of teeth to pull. Spill. Or I'm walking."

Walking. As in, he'd purposefully let the deal expire because Leo wanted to go home and sleep with his wife. He sighed. Apparently losing John Hu hadn't been enough of a wake-up call.

"I'm distracted. Sorry. It's not the proposal. Something else."

Something that needed to stop. Leo's will was ironclad and had been since he was seventeen. How had Daniella destroyed it so easily?

Dax smirked. "I should have known. You've been different since you married that woman."

He wasn't the slightest bit different. Was he?

"Watch your tone."

Friendship or not, Dax had no call to refer to Daniella as "that woman," as if Leo had hooked up with a chain-smoker in a tube top, straight from the trailer park. He'd deliberately chosen a classy, elegant woman. Not one who mirrored his childhood neighbors in the near ghetto.

Throwing up his hands dramatically, Dax flipped his gaze heavenward. "It begins. We've been through a lot of women together, my friend. What's so special about this one?"

The answer should be nothing. But it wasn't.

"I married her."

And now he was lying to his best friend. Not only was that just part of the answer, it was the tip of the iceberg. He couldn't stop thinking about her. About how beautifully she'd handled the party. Her laugh. The way she took care of things, especially him, with some kind of extrasensory perception.

When he was inside her, his world shifted. He'd never realized his world *could* be shifted. Or that he'd like its new tilt so much. That he'd willingly slide down Daniella's slippery incline.

Snorting, Dax glanced at the laptop screen positioned between their chairs and tapped on the keyboard. "So? It's not like you have feelings for her. She's a means to an end."

A vehement protest almost left his mouth unchecked. But Dax was right. Why would he protest? Daniella *was* a means to an end, like Leo had told him. It just sounded so cold from his friend's perspective. "Feelings aside, she's my wife. Not a casual date. It's important for her to be happy."

"Why? Because she might leave you? Think again. Gold diggers don't bite the hand that feeds them."

Quick-burning anger sliced through Leo's gut. "She's not a gold digger. Our marriage is beneficial to us both. You know that. Surely you don't believe it's acceptable for me to treat my wife like a dog and expect her to put up with it because I have money."

Dax quirked one eyebrow. "Like I said. This one is special."

Leo rolled his eyes. Dax saw meaning where there was none. Except they knew each other well. The Chinese food churned through Leo's stomach greasily. Or maybe that was a smear of guilt.

His track record with women spoke for itself—he wouldn't win any awards for tenderness, attentiveness or commitment. And maybe he did buy expensive presents to apologize for all of the above.

"Let's have this conversation again when *you* get married."

"Ha. That's a good one. There's no *when* in that statement. There's hardly an *if.* Women are good for one thing." Dax flashed his teeth. "They give you a reason to drink."

Perfect subject-change material. "Things not going well with Jenna?"

Too bad. Dax obviously needed someone in his life who could knock down all his commitment and trust issues. Jenna wasn't the right woman for that anyway.

"What are you talking about? She's great. The sex is fantastic." Waggling his brows, Dax leaned back in his chair. "Well, you know."

Leo's already unsettled stomach turned inside out at Dax's smarmy reference to the fact that she'd been Leo's lover first. Had Leo always treated women so casually, blowing it off as a necessary evil of success?

No. Not always. Daniella *was* special, but not the way Dax implied. Leo had treated her differently from the beginning, demonstrating a healthy respect for the institution of marriage. That's all. He was making an iceberg out of an ice cube.

Dax sat up to type out a few more corrections to the proposal. "Judging by the way you couldn't keep your eyes off Daniella at the party the other night, she must be a wildcat. Let me know if you get tired of her."

The chair's wheels squealed as Leo launched to his feet. Staring down at Dax, he crossed his arms so he didn't punch his oldest friend. "I strongly suggest you close your trap before I do it for you."

"Jeez, Leo. Calm down. She's just a woman."

"And you're just a friend." When Dax glanced up, surprise evident, Leo skewered him with a glare that couldn't possibly be misinterpreted. "Things change. Get over it."

Slowly, Dax rose to his feet. Eye to eye, they faced off and Leo didn't like the glint flashing in his friend's gaze as Dax gave Leo's stiff carriage a once-over.

"I can't believe you'd let a chick come between us. Especially not one you found through a matchmaker." Dax nearly spat the word. "Let the deal with Mastermind expire. When you come back from la-la land and realize you've lost your edge over an admittedly nice pair of boobs, I'll be around to help you pick up the pieces. We've been friends too long."

Dax stepped back and Leo let him, though his fingers were still curled into a nice, fat fist that ached to rearrange that pretty-boy face. "I agree. It's best not to go into business together right now."

"Go home to your wife," Dax called over his shoulder as he gathered his bag, phone and travel coffee mug. "I hope she's good enough in bed to help you forget how much money we just lost."

He strode out the door of Leo's conference room without a backward glance.

Sinking into the nearest chair, Leo stared out the window at the green argon lights lining the Bank of America Plaza skyscraper. Since the building housed the headquarters of Dax's far-flung media empire, the familiar outline drove the barb further into Leo's gut.

Yeah, they'd lost a lot of money. And a friendship.

He didn't imagine for a second this rift would be easily repaired. Not because of the sense of betrayal Leo felt, and not because Dax had said reprehensible things about Leo's wife.

But because Dax was right. Leo had changed since marrying Daniella. No longer could he stomach being that guy Dax described, who treated women horribly but rationalized it away and bought them shiny presents to make up for it. Or that guy who wasn't bothered by introducing an ex-girlfriend to Dax because she hadn't meant anything to him.

Dax didn't see a problem with either. Leo couldn't continue to be friends with someone who held such a low opinion of women. Why hadn't he seen that long before now? And what would it take to get Dax to recognize the problem? Maybe Dax should visit a matchmaker himself. If Elise could find the perfect woman for Leo, she could do it for anyone.

Losing the friendship hurt. Letting the deadline expire

for their proposal to Mastermind Media hurt worse. In his entire professional career, he'd never willfully given up. And one thing hadn't changed, would never change—Leo also didn't want to be that guy who lost deals or worse, lost his edge. For any reason. Let alone over a woman who drove him to distraction.

He'd lost John Hu. Now this deal. Was Tommy Garrett next?

He refused to allow that to happen. Daniella's invisible, ill-defined hold on him had to end. Immediately. He'd tried ignoring her. He'd tried sleeping at the office. He'd even tried going in the opposite direction and allowing himself small tastes of her. None of that had worked to exorcise his wife from his consciousness.

So he'd have to try the only thing left. He was going to spend the weekend in bed with Daniella in full-on immersion. By Monday, she would be out of his system and he'd have his focus back. He could share a house with her at night and forget about her during the day, like he'd planned all along.

It had to work. He'd toiled so hard to build a secure company and he owed it to everyone to maintain it. Especially Daniella. He'd vowed to care for her and he'd scrub floors at a state prison before he'd allow his wife to live next door to a meth lab like his own father had.

Ten

The book Dannie was reading held her interest about as well as the last one. Which was to say not at all. She'd parked on the settee to wait in hopes that Leo might come home soon, but it was already almost ten o'clock.

One more page. The story had to get better at some point. If it didn't, she'd get ready for bed. Leo's alarm went off before dawn and she was still adjusting to his routine.

The atmosphere shifted and she glanced up from her e-reader. Leo stood in the open doorway, one hand on the frame and the other clutching a bouquet of red roses. And he was watching her with undisguised, delicious hunger.

Heat erupted at her center and radiated outward, flushing her whole body. The e-reader fell to the carpet with a thunk, released by her suddenly nerveless fingers.

"Roses? For me?" Her voice trembled, and he didn't miss it. Her temperature rose as his expression darkened.

"In a manner of speaking." Striding to the settee, he held out his free hand and when she took it, he pulled her to her feet. His torso brushed hers and her nipples hardened. "Follow me."

Anywhere.

Mystified, she trailed him into the bathroom, where he flicked on the lights to one-quarter brightness and began filling the bathtub. Over his shoulder, he called, "It probably hasn't escaped your notice that I work a lot. I have very little opportunity to indulge in simple pleasures. So I'm correcting that oversight right now. I have this fantasy involving you, me and rose petals. This time of night, I had to buy them still attached."

He gathered the petals in one hand and wrenched them from the stalks, then released them into the water.

As the red circles floated down to rest on the surface, her heart tumbled along with them. "You have fantasies about me?"

The look on his face shot her temperature up another four thousand notches.

"Constantly."

"What am I doing in these fantasies?" she asked, her tongue nearly tripping over the words.

"Driving me pomegranates, mostly." He grinned and it was so un-Leo-like she did a double take. "By the way, I'm taking the weekend off. If you don't have other plans, I'd like to spend it with you. Maybe we could consider it a delayed honeymoon."

Honeymoon? *Weekend off?* She jammed her hands down on her hips and stared at him. "Who are you and what have you done with Leonardo Reynolds?"

His expression turned sheepish and he shrugged. "Let's say I had a revelation. We're married. I have to do things differently than I've done in the past. I *want* to do things differently," he stressed. "For you. Because you deserve it. You're a great wife."

A hard, painful lump slammed into her throat. He wanted to spend time with her. Romance her, as she'd asked. The roses were reciprocation—one great husband, coming up.

Little stabs at the corners of her eyes warned of an imminent deluge. What was he trying to do to her? She'd just become good and convinced their marriage was enough as it was. Now this.

I will not cry. I will not cry.

"You ain't seen nothing yet."

"Yeah?" He twisted the faucet handle and shut off the water. "You've been holding out on me?"

"Maybe. Talk to me about these fantasies." A good, strong dose of Leo's potent masculinity—that was what she needed to keep the emotion where it belonged. Inside. At least until she figured out where all this was coming from. Her husband had done so many about-faces she couldn't help but be slightly wary. "Have you really had a lot about me? Like what?"

"Oh, I've been so remiss, haven't I?" He tsked and sat on the edge of the garden tub, feet on the lowest step leading up to the rim. "Come here."

Her toes curled against the cold travertine as she approached and then she forgot all about a small thing like bare feet as Leo drew her between his split legs, his gaze heavy lidded with sensuous promise.

"I've been a very bad husband," he told her. "You clearly have no idea how wickedly sexy I find you. Let's correct that oversight, too, while we're at it."

Her insides disintegrated and she had no idea how she was still standing with no bones.

Slowly, he loosened each button on her blouse, widening the vee over her bra until he'd bared it entirely. The shirt slipped from her shoulders and Leo reeled in the fabric, pulling her forward.

"My fantasies are no match for the real thing." His open mouth settled onto the curve of her breast where the edge of her bra met skin. His tongue darted inside, circling her nipple. Pure, unaltered desire flared from her center, engulfing her senses.

Clutching at his shoulders, she moaned his name as he unzipped her skirt, still suckling her, wetting her bra with his ministrations. Impatiently, he peeled the cup from her breast and sucked the nipple between his teeth to scrape it lightly.

She pushed farther into his mouth and drowned in sensation as he lit her up expertly with a combination of hard teeth and magic hands against her bottom.

"Daniella," he murmured against her flesh, abrading it with slight five-o'clock shadow, which felt so amazing she shuddered.

Leo lifted his mouth and she nearly sobbed as it left her skin. He licked his lips in a slow, achingly obvious gesture designed to communicate how delicious he found her. Drinking in the sight of her pale pink bra-and-panty set, he reached around to unhook her bra, letting her breasts fall free.

He cursed, almost reverently. "Beautiful. You're the most beautiful woman I've ever seen. And you're all mine."

Her knees went numb, but his sure hands held her upright as he leaned down to kiss her waist, openmouthed, drawing her panties down simultaneously. His fingers trailed between her legs up the backside, wandering unchecked in some unknown pattern and thoroughly driving her insane.

"Leo," she choked out.

"Right here," he murmured and captured her hand. "In you go."

He led her up the stairs and into the tub, helping her lie back against the incline of the oval. She peeked up at him as he snagged a rose petal, swishing it through the water, through the valley of her breasts, around her already sensitized nipples. The motion shafted biting desire through her flesh.

When he rubbed the petal between her legs, a moan rumbled in her throat.

"Playtime is over." She yanked on his tie. "I want you in here with me."

His irises flared with dark heat.

Clothes began hitting the floor and she shamelessly watched as he revealed his taut body inch by maddeningly slow inch. A smattering of dark hair covered his chest, screaming his masculinity, and hard thighs perfectly showcased the prominent erection she wanted inside her with every shuddering breath.

He splashed into the water. The giant garden tub shrank as gorgeous, vibrant male filled it.

Leo grasped her arms and settled her into place against his chest spoon-style and immediately covered her breasts with his hands, kneading them. She gasped as his thick flesh ground hard against her rear.

Rose petals floated in the water, catching on wet skin, filling the air with their warm floral scent. He murmured wicked things in her ear as he touched her, and in combination with the warm water, his hands felt like silk against her skin, in her core, against her sensitive nub.

She reached behind her to grasp his erection. It filled her palm, hard and hot, and she caressed the slick tip. A groan ripped from deep in his chest.

He tore her hand away and clasped her hips, repositioned her and drove home in one swift stroke.

"Dannie," he whispered, his voice guttural, raw. Beautiful. It crawled inside her, filling her as surely as he filled her body. Clasping her close, he held her, torso heaving against her back as they lay joined in the water. Completed perfectly by the other.

After an eternity, he lifted her hips high enough to yank a long slice of heat from her center and eased her down again. They shuddered in pleasure together.

This *was* different. Leo was different. More focused. Drawing it out, allowing her to revel in the sensations, to feel so much more than the physical. It was a slow ride with plenty of mental scenery along the way.

Intense Leo was her new favorite and his brand of romance stole her breath.

"Dannie," he said again and increased the rhythm, hypnotically, sensuously.

He repeated her name over and over as he completed her. A dense torrent of heat gathered at the source and she split apart with a sob, not the slightest bit surprised he'd made her cry after all. She'd given him what he needed and it had been returned, tenfold.

What he'd started with the diamonds, he ended with the rose petals. She wasn't in the process of falling in love with him. It was done. Irrevocably. Wholly.

Her heart belonged to her husband.

"Leo, I…" What would he say if she told him? Surely he was in the throes, too. That's what this was all about, wasn't it? Their marriage looked different than what they'd originally thought. He wanted it to be different.

"Speechless? You?" He chuckled. "I'm incredibly flattered."

It took every ounce of Elise's personality-makeover training to bite back the words as he drained the tub and helped her out, then dried her with slow, tender swipes of a soft towel. This was too important to let Scarlett off the leash. Too important to screw up.

He'd never said he loved her. Only that he wanted to do things differently. Maybe this pseudohoneymoon was simply about sex. Goodness knew she'd given him permission to make it so often enough.

But honestly. If he didn't want her to fall in love with him, he should stop being so wonderful.

Leo threw on a robe and returned with flutes and a bottle of champagne. They drank it in bed while they talked about nothing and everything.

She kept looking for the right opening to blurt it all out. Shouldn't he know that he'd made her wildly happy? That their marriage was everything she'd ever dreamed of? Her feelings for Leo far eclipsed anything she'd ever felt for Rob. She'd found purpose and meaning in being a wife; she'd married a man who made her body and soul sing in perfect harmony and her mother was being taken care of. Leo was a sexy genie in a bottle, granting all her wishes effortlessly. She wanted to tell him.

The right moment never came.

He didn't shoot her long, lingering glances with his gaze full of love. When he took her glass and set it on the bedside table, then thoroughly ravished her, he didn't whisper the things in his heart while holding her.

Instead, he fell into a dead sleep. She lay awake, but he didn't murmur secret confessions into the darkness. Though he did seek her out while unconscious, sliding his solid thigh between hers and wrapping her up in a cloak of Leo. That part she had no difficulty understanding. He enjoyed having her in his bed. Enjoyed the closeness without the requirement of having to expose himself emotionally.

The feelings, the rush of love and tenderness, were strictly one-sided. For now.

Her marriage was *almost* everything she'd yearned for since she was a little girl. She had forty-eight hours to entice Leo that last few feet to the finish line.

When the early light of dawn through the triple bay window of the bedroom woke Leo, he didn't hesitate to indulge in another fantasy—the one he'd denied himself thus far.

He gripped Daniella's hips and wedged that sweet rear against his instant erection. His fingers trailed over her breasts and she sighed and it was sleepy. Erotic.

"Leo. It's—" One of her eyes popped open and immediately shut. "Six twenty-three. In the *morning*."

"I know." He nuzzled her neck and she arched sensuously against him. "I slept sinfully late. It's refreshing."

"Thought you were taking the weekend off," she muttered and rolled her hips expertly. The cleft between her bare cheeks sandwiched his raging erection. His eyes crossed.

"Taking the weekend off to—" She did it again. Deliberately.

"Talk a lot?" she suggested sweetly and choked on the words as he skimmed a finger through the swollen folds of her center.

Closing his eyes, he breathed in the scent of crushed roses and the musk of Daniella's arousal. "Not hardly."

He sank into her and it was amazing. There was something about spooning with her that just killed him. They fit together this way, moving in perfect cadence as they had last night, and he savored it.

All her beauty was within easy reach and he made full use of the access, tweaking her gorgeous breasts and circling her nub as he sheathed himself from behind again and again. Hot friction sparked, driving them both faster.

She climaxed with a sexy moan and he followed in a brilliant chain reaction of sensation that didn't quit.

Playing hooky from work had a lot going for it. He was slightly ashamed at how much he was enjoying his weekend off, especially given that it had essentially just started. There was a lot more indulgence to be had. A lot more fantasies to enact. A lot more dread at the imminent reel back Monday morning.

How was he going to forget Daniella and concentrate on work? It was like ordering your heart not to beat so your lungs could function.

Eventually, they rolled out of bed and he let his wife make him pancakes. It beat an energy bar by quadruple. Her coffee, as always, was amazing. He hadn't enjoyed it with her since the first time she'd made it after he fell asleep at his desk. But he never left the house without a full travel mug. Somehow it had become part of his routine to drink it on the way to work. The empty mug sat on his desk all day and the sight of it made him smile.

"What should we do with all this borrowed time?" he asked her and forked another bite into his mouth as they sat at the bistro table in the breakfast nook.

Daniella peered at him over her coffee mug. "Is that what it is? Borrowed?"

"Well…yeah." Something in her frozen posture tipped him off that he might have stumbled into quicksand. "The initiatives I have going on at the office didn't magically disappear. I'm putting them off until Monday."

"I see."

"You sound disappointed." The next bite didn't go down so well. He could stand a lot of things, but Daniella's disappointment was not one of them.

She shook her head, long brown hair rippling the way it had this morning over his shoulder. "Just trying to interpret your phrasing. *Borrowed* implies you'll have to pay it back at some point. I don't want you to have to do that."

"I made the decision to spend the weekend with you. I wanted to. Don't feel guilty."

Her eyebrows lifted. "I don't. I mean I wish you didn't have to choose. Like you've got a lot of balls to juggle and I'm the one you happened to grab."

"What other choice do I have, Daniella?" Suddenly frustrated, he dropped his fork into the middle of his half-eaten pancakes. "I have a company to run. But I'm here with you now, aren't I? I'm juggling the best I can."

It was the voice of his worst fears—that he would drop a ball. Or all of them. He was horrible at juggling.

She laughed. "Yes, you're here, but it doesn't seem like either of us are fond of the juggling. Isn't there a way to whittle down the number of balls until you can hold them all in your hand? Maybe you can hire some additional staff members or change your focus."

"You're telling me to scale back my involvement in Reynolds Capital. Take on fewer partners."

His gut clenched at the mere thought of how quickly the company would dissolve if he did what she suggested. Venture capital was a carefully constructed illusion of leveraged moving parts. Like a Jenga puzzle. Move one piece the wrong way and the whole thing crashed into an ugly pile.

"I don't know what would work best. But you do." Casually, she sipped her coffee. "Why don't you try it? Then you don't have to borrow time from work to spend it with me."

Really? She'd morphed into the opposite of an understanding wife who forgave her workaholic husband's schedule. He'd married her specifically to avoid this issue. Now she'd joined the ranks of every other woman he'd ever dated.

"*I'm* the Reynolds in Reynolds Capital. I spent a decade building the company from nothing and—" Quickly, he squashed his temper. *Give a woman an inch and forget a mile—she'll take the circumference of the Earth instead.*

"Forgive me if I overstepped. You were the one who said you wanted to do things differently and I was offering a solution. Less juggling would be different." She had the grace to smile as she covered his hand with her more delicate one. But he wasn't fooled. She had more strength in one pinky than most men did in their whole bodies. "I only meant to point out we all have choices and you make yours every day. That's all."

"Uh…" His temper fizzled. She'd only been trying to solve a problem *he'd* expressed. "Fair enough."

"Let's forget this conversation and enjoy our weekend."

Somehow, he had a feeling it wasn't going to be that simple. The die had been cast and she'd made a point with logic and style. Much to his discomfort.

True to his word, Leo didn't so much as glance at his phone or boot up his laptop once. He kept waiting for jitters to set in, like an addict deprived of his fix. The absence of being plugged in should be taking a toll. It wasn't.

He wrote it off as a keen awareness that he owed Daniella his attention until Monday morning. And then there was her gift for distraction. By midafternoon, they were naked in the warmed spa adjacent to the pool. He easily forgot about the blinking message light on his phone as they christened the spa.

He'd immersed himself in his wife's deep water and surfacing was the last thing on his mind.

So it was a bit of a shock to join Daniella in the media

room for a late movie and have her announce with no fanfare, "You need to call Tommy Garrett."

"Tommy? Why? How do you know?" Leo set down the bottle of wine and stemware he'd gone to the cellar to retrieve and pulled the corkscrew from his pocket.

"He's been trying to reach you all day. He called my cell phone, wondering if you'd been rushed to the hospital."

About a hundred things careened through his head, but first things first. "How does Tommy have your cell phone number?"

Anger flared from his gut, as shocking as it was powerful.

"Don't wave all that testosterone in my face. How do you imagine he RSVP'd for your party if he didn't have my cell phone number?" She arched a brow. "Pony Express?"

His stomach settled. Slightly. He eased the cork from the bottle and poured two glasses. Wine scraped down his throat, burning against the shame already coating it. "I'm sorry. I don't know where that comes from."

"It's okay. It makes me all gushy inside to know you care." She giggled at his expression. "The movie can wait. Call Tommy. It seemed rather urgent."

Grumbling, he went in search of his phone and found it on the counter in the kitchen. Yeah, Tommy had called a time or twelve. Four text messages, one in all caps.

He hit Callback and shook his head. Kids.

"Leo. Finally," Tommy exclaimed when the call connected. "My lawyers got all their crap straightened out. I'm going with you, man. Let's get started taking the world by storm."

Leo blindly searched for a seat. His hand hit a bar stool at the kitchen island. Good enough. "You're accepting my proposal?"

"That's what I said, isn't it? Why didn't you answer your phone, by the way?" Munching sounds filled a sudden pause. Tommy lived on Doritos and Red Bull, which

Leo always kept on hand at the office in case of impromptu meetings. Thankfully, there'd be a lot more of those in the future. "Took me forever to find Dannie's number again. I didn't save it to my contacts."

"I'm taking some…" Leo's mouth dried up and he had to force the rest. "Time off."

This was it—the Holy Grail of everything he'd worked for. Now Leo would find out if he was as good as he thought he was at selecting a winner. But not today. He'd have to sit on his hands for the rest of the weekend.

"That's cool. We can talk mañana."

It was physically painful for Leo to open his mouth and say, "It'll have to be Monday."

"Seriously?" Tommy huffed out a noise of disgust that crawled up Leo's spine. "Well, I gotta say. I'd tell you to piss off, too, if I had a woman at home like Dannie. They sure don't make many of 'em like that. I'll be by on Monday."

Leo bit his tongue. Hard. Because what could he say to refute that? Daniella *was* the reason Leo couldn't talk shop on a Sunday when normally no hour of the day or night was too sacred to pour more cement in the foundation of Reynolds Capital Management's success.

But dear God, it was difficult to swallow.

Even harder was the task of sitting next to his wife on the plush couch in the media room and *not* asking her for leeway on his promise to spend the weekend with her. He did it. Barely. And insisted Tommy's call was unimportant when she asked.

Why had he told her he was taking the whole weekend off? She would have been happy with just Saturday. It was too late now. After her speech about choices, he couldn't imagine coming right out and saying he was picking work over her.

While the movie played, Daniella emptied almost an entire bottle of wine by herself and then expressed her appreciation for the rose-petal bath the night before with a great deal of creativity. By the time the credits rolled, Leo couldn't have stated his own name under oath.

The whirlpool of Daniella had well and truly sucked him under and he could no longer pretend he was taking the weekend off for any other reason than because he physically ached when he wasn't with her.

He didn't want to pick work over her. Or vice versa. If there was a more difficult place to be than between a woman and ambition, Leo didn't want to know about it. Not just any woman, but one who tilted his world and righted it in the same breath. And not just ambition, but the culmination of banishing childhood fears and achieving adult aspirations.

Sunday, after the last round of sleepy morning indulgence Leo would permit himself to experience for a long, long time, Daniella kissed him soundly and retrieved a flat package from under the bed.

"For me?" An odd ping of pleasure pierced his chest as she nodded, handing it to him.

He tore off the plain brown wrapping to reveal a framed sepia-toned drawing.

"It's one of da Vinci's," Daniella explained quietly. "You probably know that."

He did. Reverently, he tilted the frame away from the light to reduce the glare. It was one of his favorites, a reproduction of da Vinci's earliest drawing of the Arno Valley. "The original hangs in the Uffizi. Thank you. What made you think of this?"

"Da Vinci was more than a painter. He invented. He drew. He was a sculptor and a mathematician. And, like, four other things I've forgotten." With a small laugh, she tugged the frame from his grasp and laid it on the bed, then took his hand. "He was so much more than the *Mona Lisa*. Like you're more than Reynolds Capital Management. I wanted you to know I see that."

The gift suddenly took on meaning of exponential proportions. And he wasn't sure he liked it. "Are you angling for me to show you something I drew?"

The exposure of such a thing was inconceivable. Drawing was for him alone. No one else. It would be like slicing open his brain and allowing his deepest secrets to flow out, then trying to stitch the gray matter back together. It would never heal quite right. There'd always be a scar and the secrets would be out there in the world, unprotected.

"I would have asked if that's what I was after."

"What are you after, then?"

Her expression softened. "No nefarious motives. All my motives are right here." Crossing her heart with an index finger, she sought his gaze, her irises as deep and rich as melted chocolate.

"What does that mean?"

"What do you think it means, Leo?" She smiled. "I gave you the picture because I love you and want to express that in tangible ways."

His insides shuddered to an icy halt.

I love you.

It echoed in his head, pounding at the base of his skull. Where had that *come* from? No one had ever said that to him before. Well, except his mom.

Oh, dear God. His overtly romantic mother would have a field day with this. Leo's arranged marriage had just blown up in his face. His wife had *fallen in love with him.*

What was he supposed to say in response?

"You can't drop something like that on me out of the blue."

"I can't?" She sat up, covers—and her state of undress—forgotten. "How should I have led up to it, then?"

He unstuck his tongue from the desert the roof of his mouth had turned into. "I mean, you didn't have to say it at all. That's… We're not—" He pinched the bridge of his nose and tried to corral his spooked wits before he told her the truth. That he'd liked the sound of those words far more than he would have expected. "That's not the kind of marriage we agreed to."

She recoiled and quickly composed her expression, but not before he saw the flicker of hurt. "I know that. It doesn't erase my feelings. You're a kind, generous man who makes me happy. We spent a romantic weekend together and you kind of pushed me over the edge after Tommy called and you blew him off. Wouldn't you rather I be honest with you?"

Not really, no. Not when it involved sticky emotions he couldn't fathom. Dangerous emotions. Wonderful, terrible emotions that quaked through him. Love was a hell of an indulgence and he could hardly comprehend the ramifications of her blithe announcement.

But it was out there and he couldn't ignore it. Like he couldn't ignore the corkscrew through his gut over what he had to do next. "Since you're such an advocate of honesty, I lost a couple of deals over those fantasies I couldn't get out of my head. I spent the weekend with you so I could go back to work on Monday and finally concentrate."

The pain radiating from her gaze sliced through his chest like a meat cleaver.

Get some distance before you hurt her even worse.

He couldn't reach for her. He wanted to. Wanted to tell her it was all a big lie and *I love you* was the sweetest phrase in the English language. It almost made the Tommy-free weekend worth it and that scared him the most. Because he might do it again.

Curling his fingers under, he said the most horrible thing he could think of.

"The rose petals weren't intended to seduce you into falling in love. It was an exorcism."

One that had just failed miserably. His wife had fallen in love with him. It was all over her face, in her touch. Had been for some time and he'd only just realized how much he liked it on her.

Worse, he had to pretend that her words hadn't lodged in his heart. That his soul wasn't turning them over, examining them from all angles and contemplating grabbing on with all its might. Whispering seductive ideas.

It could be like it was this weekend forever. Forget about work, not your wife. You don't have to surface. Not really.

Said Satan about the apple.

Love was the decisive destroyer of security, the ultimate quicksand that led to the ghetto, and he would not fall prey to the temptations of his weaknesses. He would not become his father. No matter how hard it was to force out the words.

"We have a marriage of convenience, Daniella. That's all."

"I understand," she whispered, and nodded once without looking up from her folded hands.

She wasn't going to slap him and storm out. The relief he'd expected to feel didn't materialize. Instead, the juggling act had grown exponentially harder. Now he had the Herculean task of continuing to push her away so she didn't utter *I love you* in his presence again. He couldn't take that raw devastation on her face, knowing that he was hurting her, knowing that he'd hurt her even more later if he slipped and said it back.

And neither would Leo allow Dax to be right. He still had his edge and that wasn't ever changing.

Eleven

The pill was so tiny. How could such small packaging prevent such a huge thing like pregnancy?

Dannie stuck the birth control pill in her mouth and swallowed, the action serving the dual purpose of getting it down her throat and keeping the tears at bay. The pill was both functional and symbolic. Not only was she preventing pregnancy, but she was giving up on grand, sweeping passion and love. Forever.

Her heart was too bruised to imagine having a baby with Leo. Not now. Maybe at some point in the future she'd get those images of him smiling tenderly at their child out of her head. Leo didn't have an ounce of tenderness in him.

Okay, that wasn't true. He had it, he just used a great deal of judiciousness in how and when he allowed it to surface. She couldn't willingly give birth to a child who would one day want his or her daddy's attention. No child deserved to be fathered by a man who refused to participate in his own life.

Scratch a baby off the list. Yet another sacrifice she'd make. She understood people didn't always get their heart's desire. But she'd about run out of dreams for her non-fairy-tale real life to strip away.

She'd had an entire weekend to show Leo how wonderful their marriage could be. And she'd failed. He didn't find the idea of opening his heart to her the least bit appealing. In her most spectacular screwup to date, she'd assumed they'd grow to care for each other. Maybe not at the same rate, but they'd eventually catch up, right? It had never occurred to her he'd refuse to show even a tiny bit of affection for his wife.

She was simply a convenience. Exactly as he'd always said. Reading unmet needs into his actions and pushing him into intimacy hadn't gotten her anywhere but brokenhearted.

Wife was her identity, her essence. Work was his. Cliché indeed.

So he went back to his sixteen-hour days and she made a doctor's appointment. After three days of falling asleep before Leo came home, the pills were unnecessary insurance thus far. Apparently telling her husband she loved him was birth control in and of itself.

The music of her stupid phone's ringtone cut the silence in the bathroom.

She glanced at it. Elise's name flashed from the screen. What in the world?

"Hello?"

"It's Elise. I'm sorry to bother you, but I'm in a bind and I need your help."

"Of course. Whatever you need, it's yours."

There was very little Dannie wouldn't do for the woman who had changed her life, broken heart notwithstanding. Elise had helped her find a secure marriage. This was the "for worse" part—so much worse than she'd predicted, and she'd expected it to *suck* if she fell in love with Leo and he didn't return her feelings.

"Thank you. So much. I've got a new applicant for the program and I'm totally booked. But I can't turn her away. Will you go through the preliminary stages with her?"

"You want *me* to teach someone else how to do her hair and makeup?"

Elise chuckled. "Don't sound so surprised. You're highly qualified."

That was only because her fairy godmother had no idea

how solidly catastrophic Dannie's match had become. "As long as it's just preliminaries. I couldn't do any of the rest."

"Oh, I'll pay you."

"I wasn't talking about that." But now she was thinking about how it was almost like a short part-time job. Good timing. That might get her mind off the empty house. "I'd do it for free."

"I insist. Can you help me out or am I imposing on your new marriage?"

Dannie bit back maniacal laughter. "I can do it. Be there in thirty minutes."

She ended the call and finished getting ready for the day. She'd stopped rolling out of bed before dawn and making Leo's coffee. What would be the point? He probably hadn't even noticed.

Elise's elegant two-story town house in uptown brought back bittersweet memories. Inside these walls, Dannie had transformed from an outspoken, penniless—and hopeless—woman into a demure, suitable wife for the man Elise's computer had matched her with.

Well, not so demure. Scarlett sometimes took over, especially when Dannie's clothes came off. And when Leo made her mad, or smiled at her or—okay, Scarlett was here to stay. Dannie sighed. The suitable part was still true. She'd orchestrated a heck of a party and Tommy had signed with Reynolds Capital. Clearly, *some* of Elise's training had taken root.

Elise answered the door and threw her arms around Dannie in an exuberant hug that knocked her off balance, despite the fact that Dannie had six inches on Elise in height. But what she lacked vertically, Elise more than made up for in personality and heart.

"Look at you," Elise gushed. "So gorgeous and sophisticated. Thanks, by the way. Come meet Juliet."

Dannie followed Elise into the living room where she'd married Leo. It seemed like aeons ago that she'd stood at that fireplace, so nervous about entering an arranged marriage she could barely speak. Never had she imagined as she slipped that ring on Leo's finger that she'd fall in love and when she told him, he'd so thoroughly reject it.

Not just reject it. He'd *exorcised* her. As if she'd been haunting Leo and he hoped to banish the grim specter of his wife from the attic in his head.

If she had known, would she have still married him? Her mother's face swam into her mind. Yeah. She would have. Her mother was too important to balk at a little thing like a broken heart.

Dannie turned her back on the fireplace.

The woman huddled on the couch unfolded and stood to greet her.

"Juliet Villere," she said and held out a hand.

Even without the slight accent, her European descent was obvious. She had that quality inherent in people from another country—it was in the style of her shoes, the foreign cut of her clothing and light brown hair, and in the set of her aquiline features.

Dannie introduced herself and smiled at the other woman. Curiosity was killing her. As Dannie did, surely Juliet had a story behind why she'd answered Elise's ad. "You're here to let Elise sprinkle some magic dust over you?"

"Magic would help."

She returned Dannie's smile, but it didn't reach her eyes and Dannie was sold. No wonder Elise hadn't turned her away. The woman radiated a forlorn aura that made Dannie want to cover her with a warm quilt and ply her with hot chocolate. And it was eighty-five degrees outside.

Elise nodded. "Juliet is a self-described tomboy. I couldn't think of anyone more ladylike than Dannie and I've already taken on more candidates than I can handle. It's a perfect match."

Heat climbed into Dannie's cheeks. She *was* ladylike when it counted. What had happened between her and Leo in the media room after he ignored Tommy's call was nobody's business but hers. Besides, he liked it when she put on her brazen side.

At least she excelled in that area of her marriage.

"Thank you for helping me, Ms. Arundel. I had nowhere else to turn." Juliet bobbed her head first at Elise and then at Dannie. "I would be grateful to find an American husband."

"Did your computer already spit out some possibles?" Dannie asked Elise.

Elise shook her head. "She's not entered yet. Makeover first, then I do the match. The computer doesn't care what you look like, but I find that the makeover gives women the confidence to answer the profile questions from the heart instead of their head. Then the algorithm matches based on personality."

"Wait." Dannie went a little faint. "External characteristics aren't part of the profile process?"

"Of course not. Love isn't based on looks."

"But…" Dannie sank onto the couch. "You matched me with Leo because he was looking for certain qualities in a wife. Organized. Sophisticated. Able to host parties and mingle with the upper crust."

Which had everything to do with external qualities. Not internal.

"Yes. That covers about four of the profile points. The rest are all related to your views on relationships. Love. Family. How you feel about sex. Conflict. You and Leo fit on all forty-seven."

"That's impossible," she countered flatly.

"Name one area where that's not true and I'll refund Leo's money right now."

"Love. I believe in it. He doesn't." Saying it out loud made it real all of a sudden and a breakdown threatened Dannie's immediate future.

"That's totally false." Elise's brow puckered as she paused. "Unless he lied on his profile. Which I suppose is possible but highly improbable."

"It can't be that foolproof."

Why was she arguing about this? The computer had matched her with Leo because they'd both agreed a marriage based on mutual goals made sense. Neither of them had expressed an interest in love from the outset and Elise was absolutely correct—Dannie had answered the profile questions from her heart. She loved her mother and marrying Leo had saved her. End of story.

"It's not. But I am." The flash of Elise's smile did not temper her self-assurance. "I administer the profile test myself and I wrote it."

Juliet watched the exchange as though it was a tennis match, eyelids shielding her thoughts. "But something is amiss or you would not be having this discussion, right?" she suggested.

Something as in Dannie had created this mess by forgetting love didn't create security, but honoring your word did. Her mother's stance on relationships had never steered her wrong before, and if she'd tried a little harder to embrace the idea of a loveless marriage, she could have avoided all this.

Elise deflated a little. "Yes, of course you're right. I'm sorry. I have to shut down my analytical side or it takes over."

Yeah, Dannie knew all about shutting down inappropriate emotional outbursts. "I'm just disappointed and mad at myself for thinking I could entice him away from his dollar signs with promises of fulfillment. It's not your fault."

Elise put a comforting hand on Dannie's arm. "My point is that you totally can. I'm sorry he's being difficult about accepting all that you have to offer beyond the ability to schedule personal appointments. But you've got what he needs emotionally, too."

Did she?

And did she have what he really needed or only what he thought he needed? For a long time, she'd smugly believed she knew the difference and her job was to guide him into understanding how to express his true desires. But really, her own pent-up needs had messed that up. And how.

Dannie took Juliet upstairs to Elise's war room, complete with a long lighted mirror and counter, racks of clothing and more hairstyling and makeup tools than a Vegas showgirl dressing room.

"All this is necessary?" Juliet's gaze darted around the room, her nostrils flaring. "What is *that*? Will it hurt?"

The panicked questions lightened Dannie's mood. "It's a straightening iron. For your hair. We don't stick your fingers between the plates unless you fail at balancing a book on your head." The other woman's cheeks blanched and Dannie laughed. "I'm kidding. Sit down in that chair and let's get started. Drink?"

Dannie crossed to the small refrigerator stocked with water, lemons, cucumbers and ice packs, the best beauty accoutrements on the planet behind a good night's sleep.

"Thank you. I'm not thirsty."

"You need to drink plenty of water. It's good for your skin and helps you stay full so you don't feel as hungry." Elise's lessons rolled out of Dannie's brain effortlessly. "Lemon gives a little bit of taste, if you prefer."

"I prefer to be sailing or swimming." The frown had no trouble reaching Juliet's eyes, unlike her smile. "I miss the water."

"Where are you from?" Dannie asked as she plugged in the hair dryer, straightening iron, curling iron and hot rollers. She hadn't decided yet how Juliet's long hair would best be styled, though it would surely benefit from a more elegant cut. And she'd definitely need a facial. Dannie mentally ticked off a few more details and realized she was humming.

It was the happiest she'd felt all week.

"South of France. Delamer." Juliet spat out the country's name as if it had the reputation of being a leper's colony instead of a Mediterranean playground for the rich and beautiful.

"That's a lovely place. And you've got those two gorgeous princes. I read that Prince Alain is getting married soon. I hope they televise it." Dannie sighed a little in what she assumed would be mutual appreciation for a dreamy, out-of-reach public figure and his royal romance.

Juliet instead burst into tears.

Dannie gathered the other woman into a wet embrace and patted her back. "Oh, honey. What's wrong?"

Juliet snuffled against her shoulder. "Matters of the heart. They can undo us like no other."

She had that right. "Is that why you left Delamer? Someone broke your heart at home?"

With one last sniff, Juliet pulled out of Dannie's arms and dragged the back of a hand under both newly steeled eyes. "I want to forget that man exists. In Delamer, it's impossible. They splash his picture on everything. If I marry an American husband, I don't have to return and watch him with his perfect princess."

Dannie finally caught up and sank into the second director's chair. "Prince Alain broke your heart?"

This story called for chocolate and lots of red wine. Unfortunately, it wasn't even lunchtime and Elise kept neither in the house.

With a nod, Juliet twirled a brush absently, her thoughts clearly thousands of miles away. "There was a scandal. It's history. I can't change it and now I have to move on. What should we do first to transform me into a woman who will attract an American husband?"

Dannie let her change the subject and spent the next two hours teaching Juliet the basics of makeup and hair. It was a challenge, as the woman had never learned an iota about either.

"If you line only the bottom lip with a pencil that's a shade darker than your lipstick, it'll create an illusion of fuller lips." Dannie demonstrated on Juliet's mouth.

"Why would I want to do that? I can't sleep in lipstick. In

the morning, my husband will realize I'm not pouty lipped, won't he?" Juliet pursed her newly painted lips and scowled at her reflection in the mirror.

"Well, figure out a way to distract him before he notices," Dannie suggested and moved on to eye-shadow techniques. There was no polite way to say Juliet needed some style.

Tomboy she was, down to her bitten-off fingernails, Mediterranean sailor's tan and split ends. The tears had unlocked something in Juliet and she talked endlessly with Dannie about her life in Delamer, minus any details about the prince.

Dannie bit back her questions, but she'd love to know how such a down-to-earth woman without an ounce of polish had gotten within five feet of royalty, let alone long enough to develop a relationship with a prince. Then there was the briefly mentioned scandal.

She didn't ask. The internet would give up the rest of the tale soon enough.

Elise checked in and offered to have lunch delivered. Since Dannie had nowhere else to be, she stayed the rest of the day. She took Juliet shopping at the Galleria in North Dallas and by the time they returned to Elise's house, Dannie had made a friend. Which, she suspected, they both desperately needed.

Before Dannie left to go back to her empty house, Elise pulled her aside. "You did a fantastic job with Juliet. If you're in the market for a permanent job, I would hire you in a second."

Dannie stared at the matchmaker. "Are you serious?"

"Totally." Elise flipped her pageboy-cut hair back. "It takes time to groom these women, and I've got more men in the computer than I ever thought possible. Successful men don't have a lot of patience for sorting out good women from bad and I provide a valuable service to them. Business is booming, in short. If you've got spare time, it would be a huge help to me."

Elise named a salary that nearly popped Dannie's eyes from their sockets. "Let me think about it."

Her job was Leo Reynolds's Wife. But suddenly, it didn't have to be. She could make money working for Elise and take care of her mother.

Leo was married to his company, first and foremost. He made that choice every day. And now, Dannie had choices, too.

She didn't want a divorce. She wanted to be Leo's wife and have the marriage of her dreams, but Leo was half of that equation. Before she made a final decision about how she'd spend the next fifty years, he should have the opportunity to fully understand what her choices were. And how they'd affect him. He might give her the final piece she needed to make up her mind.

Maybe she'd get an exorcism of her own out of it.

The exorcism was not only a colossal failure, but Leo had also learned the very uncomfortable lesson that he couldn't find a method to erase the scent of strawberries from his skin.

He'd tried four different kinds of soap. Then something called a loofah. In one of his less sane moments, sandpaper started looking very attractive. It was totally irrational. The scent couldn't actually still be there after so many days, but he sniffed and there it was. Essence of Daniella.

Leo clenched the pencil in his hand and pulled his gaze from the Dallas skyline outside his office window. The garbage can by his desk overflowed with crumpled paper. He balled the sheet on his desk and threw the latest in another round of useless brainstorming on top. It bounced out to roll under his chair. Of course. Nothing was happening as it should. Normally, paper and pencil was his go-to method when he needed to unblock.

Surprise. It wasn't working.

Tommy Garrett was very shortly going to be furious that

he'd signed with Leo instead of Moreno Partners. This deal represented the pinnacle of venture capital success and Leo's brain was fried. He had nothing to show for his half of the partnership. He was supposed to provide business expertise. Connections in manufacturing. Marketing. Ideas.

Instead he'd spent the past few days mentally embroiled in about a million more fantasies starring his wife, whom he'd deliberately driven away. For all the good it had done.

His pencil trailed across the paper and in seconds, graphite lines appeared in the form of a woman. He groaned and shut his eyes. Then opened them. What the hell. Nothing else was coming out of his brain.

As his long-suppressed muse whispered halting, undisciplined inspiration, his hand captured it, transforming the vision into the concrete. Details of Daniella's shape flowed onto the paper. Glorious. Ethereal. So beautiful his chest ached. The ache spread, squeezing his lungs and biting through muscle painfully.

Sweat broke out across the back of his neck and his hand cramped but he didn't stop. He yanked more minutiae, more emotion, from a place deep inside until he was nearly spent.

Another. More paper. Draw.

As if the drawing conjured the woman, Leo glanced up to see his wife standing in the doorway of his office. In the flesh. Dear God, Daniella was luminous in a blue dress and sky-high heels that emphasized the delicate arch to her feet.

Heart pounding, he slipped a blank sheet over the drawing and shoved everything he'd just freed back into its box. He glanced at the clock. It was eight-thirty. And dark. When had that happened?

"What are you doing here?" he asked her and stood. *Nice greeting for your wife, moron.*

"I came to see you. Do you have a few minutes?" She waltzed in as if he'd said yes.

He hadn't seen her awake since Sunday, but his body reacted as if she'd slid up against him into that niche where she fit like clinging honey instead of taking a seat on the couch in his sitting area.

"Would you like to sit down?" she offered politely, every bit the queen of the manor despite the fact that his business acumen paid the rent on this office space. Or it used to. He was this close to selling caricatures on the street if something didn't change ASAP.

He sat on the other couch. Good. Distance was good. Kept their interaction impersonal. "How are you?"

"Fine. Elise offered me a job today."

She smoothed her skirt and crossed her legs, which he watched from the corner of his eye. It was so much more powerful a blow to witness those legs sliding together when he knew what they felt like against his. What he felt like when she was near him, even when they weren't touching.

"A job? As a matchmaker?"

"As a tutor. She asked me to help her polish the women she accepts into her program. Hair, makeup. That sort of thing."

"You'd be a natural. Are you here to ask my permission? I certainly don't mind if you—"

"I'm here to ask if there's the smallest possibility you could ever love me."

A knot the size of a Buick hardened in his chest. All his carefully constructed arguments regarding the status of their relationship had ended up forming a bridge to nowhere. Probably because he could hardly convince her of it when he'd failed to convince himself.

"Daniella, we've been over this."

"No, we haven't." She clasped her hands together so tightly one of her knuckles cracked. "I told you I loved you and you freaked."

That was a pretty accurate assessment. "Well, I don't want to rehash it. We have an arranged marriage with a useful design. Let's stick with it."

"Sorry. We're rehashing it right now. Extenuating circumstances caused me to give up what I really want in a marriage. And extenuating circumstances have caused me to reevaluate. I love you and want you to love me. I need to know if we can have a marriage based on that."

I love you. Why did that settle into so many tender places inside all at once?

"You make it sound simple. It's not," he said, his voice inexplicably gruff. All the emotions drawing had dredged up weren't so easily controlled as they would have been if he'd resisted the temptation in the first place.

"Explain to me what's complicated about it."

Everything.

"You want me to choose you over my company and that's an impossible place to be."

"I'm not asking you to do that. I would never presume to take away something so important to you. Why can't you have both?"

It was the juggling-act conversation all over again. As if it was simple to just choose to have both. This would always be a problem—he saw that now. And now was the time to get her crystal clear on the subject. Get them both clear.

"I'm not built that way. I don't do anything halfway, something you might better appreciate after this past weekend. Surely you recall how thoroughly I threw myself into pleasuring you." He raked his gaze over her deliberately to make the point and a gorgeous blush rose up in her cheeks. Which made him feel worse for God knew what reason. "I went to a matchmaker to find a wife who would be happy with what I could provide financially and overlook the number of hours I put into my company. Because I don't do that halfway, either. One side is going to suffer."

All or nothing. And when it came to Daniella, he was so far away from nothing, he couldn't even *see* nothing.

Her keen gaze flitted over his expression and it wasn't difficult to pinpoint the exact instant she gleaned more than he'd intended. "But that doesn't mean you don't have feelings for me, just that you're too afraid to admit something unexpected happened between us."

"What do you want me to say, Daniella?" His voice dipped uncontrollably as he fought to keep those feelings under wraps. "That you're right? That of all the things I expected to happen in our marriage, this conversation was so far down the list it was nearly invisible?"

Her bottom lip trembled. "I want you to say what's in your heart. Or are you too afraid?"

She didn't get it. He wasn't afraid of what was in his heart; he just couldn't give in to it. The cost of loving her was too high.

"My heart is not up for discussion."

Nodding, she stood up. "Security is vitally important to me and I married you to get it. It was the only way I could guarantee my mother would be taken care of. Elise changed that today. I can support my mother on the salary she'll pay me."

An arctic chill bit into his skin, creeping through the pores to flash freeze his whole body. "Are you asking me for a divorce?"

Please, God, no.

If he lost her, it was what he deserved.

She shook her head. "I'm telling you I have a choice. And I'm making it. I took lifetime vows I plan to honor. Now I'm giving you a chance to make a choice as well as to how that marriage will look. Get off the sidelines, love me and live happily ever after. Or we'll remain married, I'll manage your personal life but I'll move back into my own room. Separate hearts, separate bedrooms. What are you going to do?"

Panic clawed at his insides, a living thing desperate to get out and not particular about how many internal organs it destroyed in its quest. She wanted something worse than a divorce. The one thing money couldn't buy—him. His time. His attention. His love.

"That's ridiculous," he burst out and clamped his mouth closed until he could control what came out of it. "I told you what I need, which is for you to be happy with what I can give. Like I've told you from the very beginning. You're throwing that back at me, drawing a line. You or Reynolds Capital Management."

A tear tracked down her cheek. "Don't you see, Leo? *You* drew that line. Not me."

"My mistake. The line you drew is the one where you said I can't sleep with you anymore unless I'm in love with you."

"Yes. That is my fault." Her head dropped and it took an enormous amount of will to keep from enfolding her in his arms. But he was the source of her pain, not the solution. "My mother…she's an amazing woman, but she has a very jaded view of marriage and I let it fool me into believing I could be happy with a loveless arrangement. And I probably would have been if you were someone different. Someone I couldn't love. Be the husband I need, Leo."

She raised her head and what he saw in the depths of her shiny eyes nearly put him on his knees, prostrate before her in desperate apology, babbling, "Yes, I will be that husband," or worse, telling her he'd do anything as long as she'd look at him like that forever: as though he was worthy of being loved, even though he'd rejected her over and over again.

The overflowing trash can taunted him.

Lack of focus is what happens when you let your wife swallow you. Other venture capital firms have fewer dominoes, more liquid assets, less leveraged cash. One push and it'll all vanish.

He could never do what she was asking.

Once and for all, he could resolve it. Right here, right now, give her that final push away before he gave in to the emotions and forgot all the reasons he couldn't have his company *and* love Daniella.

"I stay on the sidelines for a reason. It's how I balance my obsessive personality." His heart thumped painfully. This was the right thing, for him and Reynolds Capital. Why didn't it feel like it? "I need you to be the wife I thought I was getting from EA International."

Which was impossible. Daniella could never be the out-of-sight, out-of-mind wife he'd envisioned. He'd given up on categorizing her and forcing her into a box when she insisted on being in all the boxes simultaneously. His multi-talented wife was the only woman alive who could do that.

Her expression went as stiff as her spine. "Then that's what you'll get. I'll schedule your appointments and host your parties and make you look good to your associates. I won't be in your bed at night, but I'll give you a hundred percent during the day and never mention how many hours you work."

It was everything he'd asked for. And the polar opposite of what he wanted. He vised his throbbing temples between his middle finger and his thumb but his brain still felt as though it was about to explode. How had she managed to twist this around so that they were back to their original agreement but it felt as if she'd kicked him in the stomach?

"I wish…" She crossed her arms as if holding herself in. "Love creates security, too. I wish you could see that. But if it's your choice for me to be nothing more than a glorified personal assistant, I hope it makes you happy. Just keep in mind that your company *and* your wife bear your name. You will always be a part of both."

And then she walked out, heels clicking on the stained concrete in perfect rhythm to the sound of his soul splitting in two.

Twelve

"Dorito?" Tommy offered and stuck out the bag.

Leo shook his head. Doritos didn't sit well on an empty stomach. Nothing sat well on an empty stomach, especially not the dreck in his coffee cup. Mrs. Gordon had remade it four times already and the look on her face said he'd better be happy with this round.

He shoved the half-full mug to the far end of the conference table, wished it was a travel mug filled by his wife and scrubbed his jaw. Rough stubble stabbed his fingers. *Forgot to shave. Again.*

"So, amigo." Tommy crunched absently and nodded to the TV on the wall, where Leo's laptop screen was displayed. "I've redone this schematic twice. The prototype passed the CAD analysis. What's it going to take to get you happy with it?"

Hell would probably freeze over before Leo was happy about anything. He'd officially labeled this funk Daniella's Curse, because until she'd said she hoped his choice made him happy, he'd never given a thought to whether he was or not. And this funk was the opposite of happy.

He missed his wife. Her invisible presence invaded every last area of his life, including his car, which never dipped below half a tank of gas. And smelled like strawberries.

"The schematic is still wrong. That's why I keep telling you to redo it." Leo flipped the drawing vertically inside the CAD program and glanced up at the TV. "Look, you can't take this to manufacturing as is. We have to shave another two cubic centimeters somewhere to meet the price point. Otherwise the markup will be too high and the distribution deals will fall through."

Leo's phone beeped. Daniella's picture flashed and he snatched it up. Text message. He frowned at the concisely worded reminder of his appointment for a haircut that afternoon. Of course she hadn't called to talk to him.

"Why does this have to be so complicated?" Tommy complained. "I designed the thing. That should be enough. Why don't *you* figure out where to shave off whatever you think makes sense?"

Leo fiddled with the pencil in his fingers, weaving it through them like a baton, and counted all the way to fifteen for good measure. It did not calm him. "You're the designer. You have to redesign when it's not ready." His fingers sought the leather portfolio on the table. The picture he'd drawn of Daniella was inside. It equaled serenity in the midst of turmoil. Oddly enough. "I help you on the back end. We've been over this."

Shades of the last real conversation he'd had with Daniella filtered through his mind. Why did he have to constantly remind people of things they should already know? Leo had a specific role to fill—in the background. Always. Nobody remembered that he stayed out of the middle, except him.

"I don't know how to get it to your specifications!" Tommy burst out in recalcitrant five-year-old fashion, complete with a scowl and crossed arms. "I've tried. I need help. That's why I signed with you."

"I'm your financial backer. I'm only talking to you about the schematic now because we're behind schedule and I need a good design today." With a short laugh, Leo shook his head. "Why would you assume I could do anything to help?"

Tommy flipped hair out of his face. "Dannie. She believes in you. She totally convinced me you walk on water daily and in your spare time you invest in people's potential. As far as she's concerned, you're the messiah of everything."

His gut spasmed. What exactly had his wife told Tommy to give him such a ridiculous picture of Leo? "That's entirely too fanciful for what I do."

Entirely too fanciful for a mortal man who'd made plenty of mistakes. But it didn't stop the low hum of pleasure behind his rib cage. Did Daniella really think of him like that, as someone heroic and unfailing? Or had she said those things for Tommy's benefit, playing her part as a dutiful wife?

Leo had the distinct, uncomfortable realization it was probably both. And he didn't deserve either.

Eyebrows raised, Tommy crossed his feet casually. "Yeah? If you tell me you don't know exactly what needs to happen with that schematic, I'll call you a dirty liar. You've been trying to lead me to it for an hour and I can't see it."

Leo sighed and thought seriously about driving the pencil through the table, but it would only break the wood, not solve his mounting frustration. Before he could count the reasons why it was a stupid, ridiculous path, he centered a piece of paper under the graphite and drew the first line.

Tommy's purple high-tops hit the floor as he leaned forward to peer over Leo's shoulder. The fuel-converter schematic took shape on the paper. With each new line, he explained to Tommy where he varied from the original design, why the modification was necessary, what the downstream manufacturing effect would be.

Occasionally Tommy interjected questions, objections and once, a really heartfelt "Dude. That's righteous."

One of Tommy's objections was sound and Leo reconsidered his stance on it. He erased that part of the drawing and incorporated Tommy's suggestion. Mrs. Gordon left for the day, shaking her head and mumbling about creative minds. After several hours, many heated exchanges and a few moments of near-poetic collaboration, they had a design they could both live with.

The last time Leo could honestly say he'd had that much fun was during the weekend he'd spent with Daniella. Before that—never.

Once Leo had scanned the finished product into his laptop and displayed it on the TV, Tommy whistled. "A work of art. I have to use every tool known to designers to put something that beautiful together. I can't believe you freehanded that. With a pencil, no less."

"A pencil gets the shading right," Leo muttered with a shrug. "I guess you could say it's a talent."

"I knew you had it in you," Tommy said smugly. "If I'd gone with Moreno Partners, I'd be screwed right now. Kiss your wife for me. She knows her stuff."

If only. Ironically, his current interaction with Daniella wasn't too different from how their marriage had started out, before they'd begun sharing a bedroom. If she hadn't barged in and demanded he start sleeping with her, would they still be exchanging text messages with no clue how much more there could be between them?

"She does have some kind of extrasensory perception," Leo said. "I'm afraid she's the one who walks on water."

No, *he'd* be clueless. She wouldn't. From the beginning, she'd seen possibilities, pushing their relationship into realms deeper and stronger than he'd ever imagined could be between any two people, let alone when one of them was Leo Reynolds.

How had that happened when he wasn't looking? And why did the loss of something he'd never asked for haunt him?

He'd done everything he could to drive her away so she wouldn't be hurt and instead of leaving him, his wife had stayed. Why didn't she get the message already?

With a grin, Tommy nodded vigorously. "Dannie's awesome."

His wife's nickname lodged in his gut, spreading nasty poison.

Leo liked Tommy. He was enthusiastic, tireless, brilliant. So what was it about Tommy simply saying his wife's name that burned Leo up? It was more than jealousy, more than a fear either Tommy or Daniella had less than pure intentions toward each other.

It was because Tommy held up a mirror and Leo hated his reflection.

This Dorito-crunching, Red Bull–slurping wonder kid was a younger, unrestricted, better version of Leo. Tommy could call a woman Dannie and think nothing of it, whereas Leo couldn't descend into that kind of intimacy unless he was drunk on Daniella's powerful chemistry.

And he wished he could be more like Tommy.

Tommy polished off the bag of Doritos. "You're awesome, too. I'm over here soaking it all up like SpongeBob."

A cleansing laugh burst out of Leo's mouth, unchecked. "Thanks. It's nice to have an appreciative audience."

"Dude, you talk and I'll listen, no matter what you say. I'm in awe of you right now. I think I learned more today than I did in four years at Yale. What else can you teach me?"

Oh, no. That was beyond the realm of his role. He and Tommy were financial partners, with a carefully constructed agreement separating their interests into neat boxes. That should be the extent of their relationship.

Should be. Everything should fit into a neat box. And nothing did, despite all of Leo's efforts.

"What do you want to know?"

With a lusty sigh, Tommy grinned. "Everything. Lay it on me."

And that was it. For the first time in his life, Leo had become an in-the-flesh mentor and for whatever reason, it felt right. It was a connection with his profit margin, one he'd never explored but suddenly wanted to.

All business is personal.

His wife had pointed that out long ago and he'd brushed it off as foolish sentiment. But it suddenly made brilliant sense. He hadn't lost the deal for Mastermind Media because he'd lost his edge, but because he'd willfully chosen not to enter into a partnership with Dax, for whom he'd lost a great deal of respect. His relationship with Daniella merely highlighted it, but hadn't caused it.

Leo's relationship with Daniella shone into all of his corners and scared away the excuses, the fears. She hadn't left him because she'd already figured out what Leo should have seen long ago.

Their arrangement was dead. Now they had an opportunity to make their marriage something else.

Instead of being like Tommy, maybe Leo should be a better version of himself. One that could be worthy of a woman like Daniella Reynolds.

Leo's morose mood lightened. After setting aside two afternoons a week for Tommy to bring his best SpongeBob absorption skills, Leo kicked his new disciple out of his office so he could leave.

When he got home, Leo paused outside Daniella's closed bedroom door and placed his palm flat against it, as he did every night. Sometimes he imagined he could feel her breathing through the door. The scent of strawberries lingered in the hall, wrapping around him.

He'd built this home as a fortress, a place that represented all the stability he'd never had as a child. Daniella had become an inseparable part of that. How could he ever have lived here without her? How could he explain to her what value she'd brought to his life?

Guilt gnawed a new hole in his gut. She deserved so much more than what he'd given her.

She should have left him.

The main goal of marriage was security. Odd how he

felt as though the ground was disappearing beneath him at an alarming pace the longer he had a wife in name only.

Instead of standing there like a stalker, he knocked and shifted the bulky package in his hand before him like a peace offering. He prayed it might change things but he had no clue how, or what that change might look like.

He just knew he couldn't do marriage like this anymore. The ball was in his court. Had been the entire time. Hopefully he'd picked up the proper racket.

Daniella opened the door, shiny hair down around her face and clad in a skintight tank top and loose pajama bottoms with her flat midriff peeking through. The swift, hard punch to his solar plexus nearly rendered him speechless.

Somehow he managed to choke out, "Hi."

Her luminous brown eyes sought his and a wealth of unexpressed things poured from them. "Hi."

"A gift. For you." He handed her the wrapped package and laced his fingers behind his back before he pulled her into an embrace she probably wouldn't welcome. But oh, dear God, did he want to touch her. "You gave me one. I'm returning the favor."

She ripped it open and his thudding heart deafened him as he waited.

Silently, she evaluated the basket of pomegranates. "What does this mean?"

She tilted the basket as if to show him, which was unnecessary. He'd placed each one in the basket himself, positioning it just so to interlock with the others. "You're still driving me pomegranates. Sleeping in separate bedrooms hasn't changed that."

The tension spiraled between them, squeezing his lungs, and he smiled in hopes of loosening it.

"I got that part. *Why* are you giving them to me?" Her gaze probed his, challenging him and killing his smile. She wasn't going to make this easy. She always had before, using her special powers to figure out exactly how to help him navigate.

Not this time. He shifted from foot to foot but couldn't find a comfortable stance. "Because I wanted to give you something that had special significance."

Her expression didn't change. "So it's nothing more than a gift designed to buy your way out of giving me anything emotional."

What did she want from him? A pound of flesh? She held in her hands one of the most emotional things he'd ever done. Somehow he had to make her see that.

"It's not just a gift, like jewelry. It's better than that."

Frozen, she stared at him for an eternity, long enough for him to realize he'd devalued the diamonds he'd given her for the party. Which were in her earlobes at this moment.

This was not going at all how he'd envisioned. She was supposed to make the first move. Fall into his arms and tell him this separation was killing her, too.

At the very least, she should be giving him a choice between two impossible options and then pretending it was okay when he picked the wrong one. The way she always did.

Floundering, he cast about for a lifeboat. "I'm sorry. I didn't mean it that way."

"How did you mean it? Or do you even know?"

"I do know!" At her raised eyebrows, he faltered. It had been an off-the-cuff protest. And a lie. Nothing between them was tangible. Or quantifiable. Which made it impossible to define the bottom line.

This was like a bad joke. What did the guy who had never hung on to a woman longer than a few weeks say to his wife? If only she'd tell him the punch line, they could move past this.

"What do you want me to say?"

"That's for you to figure out. I'll be here when you do. Thank you for the pomegranates."

With that, she closed the door in his face. Because at the end of the day, she knew the truth as well as he did. Jewelry. Pomegranates. Same difference. He still hadn't given her the one thing she really wanted—everything.

If he truly hoped to change their marriage, he had to dig much deeper. And it was going to hurt.

Dannie slid to the ground, the wood of her door biting into her back, and muffled a sob against the heel of her hand. *Pomegranates.*

Why did this have to be so hard?

Her mother was right: love was the stupidest thing of all to base a marriage on. It hurt too much. All Leo had to do was say, "I brought you a gift because I love you."

If his inability to do so wasn't bad enough, she had the awful feeling that the basket was indeed symbolic of his inner turmoil. Only supreme will suppressed her desire to knuckle under.

He'd tried. He really had. It just wasn't good enough, not anymore. Once upon a time, she'd believed they were a good match because they both valued security. It was how they went about achieving it where they differed.

Leo was an intense, focused man who cut himself off from people not because he didn't want to invest emotionally, but as some kind of compensation for what he viewed as a shortcoming of his personality. She couldn't spend a lifetime pretending it was okay that he refused to dive headlong into the game. She'd already compromised to the point of pain.

His mother had warned her how challenging Leo would be to love. Dannie should get a medal. So should Leo's mother.

Sleep did not come easily. She glanced at the time, convinced she'd been lying there for an hour but in reality, only four minutes had passed since the last clock check. She gave up at quarter past two and flipped on the TV to watch a fascinating documentary about the Civil War.

Her favorite historical time period unfolded on the screen. Women in lush hoopskirts danced a quadrille in the Old South before everything fell apart at the hands of General Sherman cutting a swath through Georgia on his way to the sea.

Dannie's heart felt as if it had taken a few rounds from a Yankee musket, too.

But where Scarlett O'Hara had raised a fist to the sky and vowed to persevere, Dannie felt like giving up.

A divorce would be easier. She could take care of her mother, live with Elise and try to forget about the man she'd married who refused to get out from behind the scenes.

But she'd taken vows. Her stomach ached at the thought of going back on her word. Her heart ached over the idea of staying. Which was worse?

All she knew was that she couldn't do this anymore.

In the morning, she took a bleary-eyed shower and spent the day at Elise's working with Juliet. They were both subdued and honestly, Dannie didn't see the point in giving Juliet a makeover when the woman was already beautiful. Besides, it wasn't as though a manicure and hot rollers would give Juliet what she most desired.

Or would it?

"What if your match is someone you can't fall in love with? Would you still marry him?" Dannie asked Juliet as she showed her how to pin the hot roller in place against her scalp. Some people didn't care about love. Some people found happiness and fulfillment in their own pursuits instead of through their husbands.

But Dannie wasn't some people, and she'd lied to herself about which side of the fence she was on, embracing her mother's philosophy as if it were her own.

Juliet made a face. "I would marry a warthog if he had

the means to keep me in America. Arranged marriages are common in Europe. You learn to coexist."

"But is it worth it to become someone else in order to have that means?"

The other woman shot her puzzled glance in the mirror. "I'm still me. With fingernails." She stuck out a hand, where a nail technician had created works of art with acrylic extensions.

Dannie glanced at her own reflection in the mirror. She'd been polished for so long, it was no longer a shock to see the elegant, sophisticated Mrs. Reynolds in the glass instead of Dannie White. Except they were one and the same, with a dash of Scarlett.

Elise had done the makeover first, but the computer had matched her to Leo because she was perfect for him. As she was. Not because Elise had infused Dannie with some special magic and transformed her into someone Leo would like.

I'm still me, too, but better.

Leo provided the foundation for her to excel as his wife and let her be as brazen, outspoken and blunt as she wanted. He was okay with Dannie being herself.

Their personalities were the match. She'd heard it over and over but today, it clicked.

She'd been so focused on whether Leo would kick her out if she screwed up it had blinded her to the real problem. They both had come into this marriage seeking security, but struggled with what they said they wanted versus what they'd actually gotten. And they were *both* trying to balance aspects of their incredibly strong personalities *for no reason.*

They wanted the same thing deep in their hearts—the security of an unending bond so strong it could never be broken.

The open-heart lavaliere around her neck caught the light as she leaned over Juliet's shoulder to arrange her hair. Elise had given Dannie the necklace when she'd agreed to marry Leo, as a gift between friends, she'd assumed.

Now she saw it as a reminder that marriage required exactly that—*two* open hearts.

Had she been too harsh with Leo about the pomegranates? Maybe she should find a way to coexist that didn't involve such absolutes. Security was enough for Juliet. A fulfilling partnership had been enough for Dannie once.

She'd pushed intimacy in an attempt to fulfill Leo's unvoiced needs and ignored the need he'd actually voiced— a wife he could depend on, who would stick with him, no matter what. Even through the pain of a one-sided grand, sweeping love affair.

One thing was for sure. Real life wasn't a fairy tale, but Dannie wanted her happily ever after anyway. Cinderella might have had some help from her fairy godmother, but in the end, she'd walked into that ball with only her brain and a strong drive to make her life better. What was a fairy tale but a story of perseverance, courage and choices?

It was time to be the wife Leo said he needed, not the one she assumed he needed.

Leo's car was in the garage when Dannie got home. She eyed it warily and glanced at her watch. It was three o'clock on a Tuesday. Someone had died. Someone *had* to have died.

Dannie dashed into the house, a lump in her throat as she triple checked her phone. She'd have a call if it was her mother. Wouldn't she?

"Leo!" Her shout echoed in the foyer but he didn't answer.

The study was empty. Her stomach flipped. Now she was really scared.

Neither was he in the pool, the kitchen, the media room, the servants' quarters around the back side of the garage or the workout room over the garage.

Dannie tore off two nails in her haste to turn the knob on

his bedroom door, the last threshold she should ever cross, but he could be lying a pool of his own blood and need help.

Curtains blocked the outside sunlight and the room was dark but for the lone lamp on Leo's dresser. It shone down on him. He sat on the carpet, hunched over a long piece of paper resting on a length of cardboard. Clawlike, he gripped a pencil in his hand, stroking it over the paper swiftly.

"Leo?" She paused just inside the door frame. "Are you okay?"

He glanced up. The light threw his ravaged face into relief, shadowing half of it. "I don't know when to stop. I tried to tell you."

"Tell me what? What are you talking about? What do you need to stop?"

"Drawing." He flipped a limp hand toward the room at large and that's when she realized white papers covered nearly every surface.

"How long have you been in here?" There were hundreds of drawings, slashes and fine lines filling the pages with a mess of shapes she couldn't make out in the semidark. *Hundreds.* Apparently she'd massively misconstrued what he meant by not doing things halfway.

"Since the pomegranates." His voice trembled with what had to be fatigue. He'd been holed up in here since last night?

"But your car was gone this morning."

"Needed a pencil sharpener. Is it enough? Look at the pictures, Daniella. Tell me if it's enough."

Her heart fluttered into her throat. "You want me to see your drawings?"

In response, he gathered a handful and clambered to his feet to bring them to her. The half light glinted off the short stubble lining his jaw and dark hair swept his collar. Not only had he skipped the haircut she'd scheduled, but he'd obviously not shaved in several days. His shirt was untucked and unbuttoned and this undone version of Leo had a devastating, intense edge.

As if presenting a broken baby bird, he gingerly handed off the drawings and waited silently.

She glanced at the first one and every ounce of oxygen in the room vanished.

"It's you," she whispered. She flipped through the pages. "They're all of you."

Gorgeously rendered. Drawn by the hand of a master who knew himself intimately and who was unashamed to show the world all the glorious details of what made up Leonardo Reynolds.

And he was completely naked in every single one.

He shut his eyes. "I stripped myself bare. Emotionally, physically, spiritually. For you. I cannot possibly explain what it cost me to put all of it on the paper. But it's there. Tell me it's enough."

Oh, my God.

"Leo," she croaked through a throat suddenly tight with unshed tears. This had all been for her. "Yes. *Yes.* It's enough."

More than enough. She clutched the pages to her abdomen. It was the deepest expression of his love she could possibly imagine and these pictures were worth far more than a thousand words. They told the story she'd yearned to hear, lifting his shell once and for all, revealing everything important about the man she loved.

Artist Leo touched her deep in her soul with invisible, precious fingers.

He deflated, almost collapsing. But then he opened his eyes and caught her in his arms, binding her to his strong, solid body. Her knees weren't too steady either as she let the drawings flutter to the floor and burrowed up against him.

Warm. Beautiful. Hers.

Her brain was having trouble spitting out anything coherent. And then he kissed her and she stopped thinking at all.

It was hungry, openmouthed, sloppy and so powerful. As he kissed her, he mouthed words she couldn't understand.

He broke away and murmured into her hair. And the phrase crystallized. "I want to be the husband you need."

"Oh, darling, you are." In every sense. He had been from the first moment, providing a safe, secure place for her to bloom into his wife. He was her match every bit as much as she was his.

He shook his head. "I haven't been. I don't deserve you. But I want you. So much."

"You have me. Forever. We're married, remember?" She smiled but he didn't return it.

"Not like this. No more agreement. No separate bedrooms. No separate hearts." He put his palm flat against his breastbone like a pledge. "I could've hired a personal assistant. But I didn't. I went looking for a wife because I needed one. I need a wife who sees past all my faults and loves me anyway. It's not too late, is it?"

She placed her palm on top of his. "Never. But, Leo, you didn't go to work today. You're not throwing away your company's success for me. I won't let you."

"I can't—so tired." His knees buckled and he fell to the carpet, taking her with him. He pulled her into his lap and cupped her jaw in his strong hands, fiercely, passionately, as if he'd never let go. "Like you said. You didn't draw the line. I did. It's what I do."

With a lopsided half smile, he jerked his head at the hundreds of drawings decorating the bedroom behind him. "You weren't trying to force me to make impossible choices. The choices weren't yours to present. You were simply helping me see what options had been there all along. Reynolds Capital Management is a part of me I can't give up. So are you."

"You want both? Me and your company?" Hope warred with reality. The drawings were a big, flashing exhibit A of what happened when Leo focused on something. His preferred spot on the sidelines made troubling sense.

"I want it all." His eyes closed for a beat, a habit she'd noticed he fell into when he struggled with what was going on inside. "I don't know how to balance. But I want to. I have to try."

His voice broke, carving indelible lines in her heart.

This was the open, raw, amazing man she'd fallen in love with. But she and Leo were the same, with facets of their personality that weren't always easy to manage.

"You can do it. We'll do it together." Who better to help him figure it out than the woman standing behind him, supporting him? "I love your intensity and I don't ever want you to feel like you can't be you. If you want to hole up on a Saturday because you've got a hot new investment opportunity to work, do it. Just don't expect to get much sleep that night. Don't ever deny any piece of yourself. I need all of you. As long as we both shall live."

Her job as Mrs. Reynolds was so simple: provide a foundation for him to blossom, the way he'd done for her.

"That sounds promising. If I have to work on a Saturday, will you still make me coffee?" he asked hopefully.

She smiled. "Every time. We'll both give a little and balance will come."

Nodding slowly, he cleared his throat. "I think it must be like when you have children. You love one with all your heart. Then another one comes along. Somehow you make room. Because it's worth it."

Children. Leo was talking about having children in the same breath with trying to balance.

The tears gathered in earnest this time. He'd transformed before her very eyes, but instead of a pirate or Rhett Butler or even a battered Mr. Fourpaws before her, he was wholly Leonardo and 100 percent the love of her life. "Yeah. I think it must be like that. We have stretchy hearts."

"Mine's pretty full. Of you." He was kissing her again

like a starving man, murmuring, but this time, she had no trouble deciphering what he was saying—*I love you*.

Then he said, "My hand hurts."

She laughed as she kissed it. "Wait right here. I have pills to throw in the trash and a red-hot wedding night outfit to wear for you. I guarantee you'll forget all about your sore hand."

Technically, it wasn't her wedding night. But in her book, every night was her wedding night when she was married to a man who loved her as much as Leo.

Epilogue

Leo Reynolds wished he could marry his wife, but they were already married and Daniella refused to divorce him just so he could have the fun of proposing to her in some elaborate fashion.

"Come on, you can't fool me," Leo teased her as they gripped the railing of the observation deck on the third level of the Eiffel Tower. Nine hundred feet below, the city of Paris spread as far as the eye could see. "You missed out on the proposal *and* the wedding of your dreams. You wouldn't like to do it all over again?"

Daniella kissed his cheek with a saucy smile, throwing her loose brown hair over her shoulder. "I'm getting the honeymoon of my dreams. And the husband. All that other stuff pales in comparison."

Sure it did. His wife suffered from an affliction with no cure—overt romanticism. Since he loved her beyond measure, he took personal responsibility for ensuring she never lost it. "Then you'll have to forgive me when I do something pale and lackluster like…this."

He slipped the ring box from his pocket and popped it open to reveal the rare red diamond ring inside. "Daniella Reynolds, I love you. Will you promise to be my wife the rest of our days, always wear that sexy lingerie set and let me make you as happy as you've made me?"

Daniella gasped. "Oh, Leo. I love you, too, and of course I promise that, with or without a ring. But it's beautiful."

"It's one of a kind. Like you. This ring is symbolic of a different sort of marriage, one based on love. The one I want with you. Every time I see it on you, I'll think about how love is the best security and how easily I could have lost it." He pulled the ring from its nest of velvet and gripped his wife's hand, slipping it on her third finger to rest against her wedding ring. And then he grinned. "Plus, the stone is the same color as pomegranates."

A tear slipped down her cheek at the same moment she laughed. "Thank you. Paris was enough but this…" She stuck her hand out and tilted it to admire the ring. "This is amazing. When in the world did you find time to shop for jewelry? You've been cramming for Tommy's product launch for weeks so you could squeeze in this trip."

"Tommy came with me and we strategized in between." Leo rolled his eyes. "Trust me, he was thrilled to be involved. I never imagined when he said he wanted to learn everything that would include how to pick out a diamond for a woman."

Daniella giggled. "With you as his mentor, I'm sure he'll make the future love of his life very happy."

Tommy had trashed Leo's original proposal. Garrett-Reynolds Engineering opened its doors that same week and the payoff for becoming full partners had been immeasurable. Not only did Leo have a lot of fun, but for the first time, his profit flowed directly from his hand instead of via carefully constructed financing agreements. Leo was right in the middle of every aspect of the business and it fulfilled him in ways he could never completely comprehend.

Without Daniella, he never would have taken that step. She'd invested in his potential and given him a makeover from the inside out. He'd gladly spend the rest of his life loving her for it.

"How're things going in there?" Leo spread his hand across Daniella's abdomen and the thought of their child eventually being inside tightened his throat with awe and tenderness.

"Not pregnant yet. Though certainly not from lack of trying." Her grin warmed his heart. Everything about her warmed his heart, touching him in places he didn't even know existed. "It's only a matter of time."

"We must try harder. I insist."

A baby was one of many possibilities he eagerly anticipated, owing to his new perspective on marriage. And life in general.

Leo kissed his wife and it felt like the beginning of something that would take a very long time to finish—forever.

* * * * *

Don't miss the next two books in the
HAPPILY EVER AFTER, INC. *trilogy*
from Kat Cantrell:

MATCHED TO A PRINCE
Available August 2014

MATCHED TO HER RIVAL
Available September 2014

If you liked this marriage of convenience tale,
you'll love Kat Cantrell's

MARRIAGE WITH BENEFITS

Available now, from Harlequin Desire!

COMING NEXT MONTH FROM

HARLEQUIN

Desire

Available August 5, 2014

#2317 THE FIANCÉE CAPER
by Maureen Child
When ex-cop Marie blackmails reformed jewel thief Gianni Coretti into helping her, she expects the sexy Italian to cooperate—not to suggest they go undercover together as bride and groom!

#2318 TAMING THE TAKEOVER TYCOON
Dynasties: The Lassiters • by Robyn Grady
Can good girl Becca Stevens, head of the Lassiters' charitable foundation, keep corporate raider Jack Reed from destroying the family's empire—and win his heart in the bargain?

#2319 THE NANNY PROPOSITION
Billionaires and Babies • by Rachel Bailey
New mom and princess-on-the-run Jenna Peters hides out as a nanny, only to fall for single dad Liam. But will he trust in the passion they've found when her true identity is revealed?

#2320 REDEEMING THE CEO COWBOY
The Slades of Sunset Ranch • by Charlene Sands
Busy raising her infant niece, Susanna is strictly off-limits when her former flame Casey comes back to town. But this rodeo star turned CEO knows no limits...especially when it comes to one very irresistible woman.

#2321 MATCHED TO A PRINCE
Happily Ever After, Inc. • by Kat Cantrell
When a matchmaker pairs Prince Alain with his ex, the scandalous commoner Juliet, he refuses to forgive and forget...and then they're stranded on a deserted island together and old sparks reignite!

#2322 A BRIDE'S TANGLED VOWS
by Dani Wade
Forced to marry for the family business, Aiden Blackstone is surprised by his attraction to his bride. But when someone sabotages his inheritance, can he trust the woman he's let into his bed—and his heart?

YOU CAN FIND MORE INFORMATION ON UPCOMING HARLEQUIN® TITLES, FREE EXCERPTS AND MORE AT WWW.HARLEQUIN.COM.

HDCNM0714

REQUEST YOUR FREE BOOKS!
2 FREE NOVELS PLUS 2 FREE GIFTS!